Churchill, Jill

A groom with a view

$22.00

DATE			
11-19			
2-3			
9-22			
10-10			

A GROOM WITH A VIEW

A GROOM WITH A VIEW

Other Jane Jeffry Mysteries by
Jill Churchill
from Avon Books

GRIME AND PUNISHMENT
A FAREWELL TO YARNS
A QUICHE BEFORE DYING
THE CLASS MENAGERIE
A KNIFE TO REMEMBER
FROM HERE TO PATERNITY
SILENCE OF THE HAMS
WAR AND PEAS
FEAR OF FRYING
THE MERCHANT OF MENANCE

A GROOM WITH A VIEW

A JANE JEFFRY MYSTERY

JILL CHURCHILL

This is a work of fiction. Names, characters, places, and incidents either are the product of the author's imagination or are used fictitiously. Any resemblance to actual events, locales, organizations, or persons, living or dead, is entirely coincidental and beyond the intent of either the author or the publisher.

AVON BOOKS, INC.
1350 Avenue of the Americas
New York, New York 10019

Interior design by Kellan Peck
Jill Churchill can be reached by e-mail at **cozybooks@aol.com**
ISBN: 0-380-97570-X

Library of Congress Cataloging in Publication Data:
Churchill, Jill.
A groom with a view : a Jane Jeffry mystery / Jill Churchill. —1st ed.
p. cm.
PS3553.H85G7 1999 99-16666
813'.54—dc21 CIP

First Avon Twilight Printing: October 1999

Printed in the U.S.A.

FIRST EDITION

QPM 10 9 8 7 6 5 4 3 2 1

www.avonbooks.com/twilight

A GROOM WITH A VIEW

Prologue

"**Do you know** Livvy Thatcher?" Jane Jeffry asked her best friend Shelley Nowack.

"Let me in out of the cold and I'll tell you," Shelley said.

Shelley had run over to Jane's house from her own, which was next door. She hadn't bothered to put on a coat for such a short jaunt and was already freezing. She stepped into Jane's warm kitchen and shivered dramatically. "I've lived in the Chicago area all my life," Shelley griped, "and every January I ask myself why a sane person would stay here *on purpose.* It's not a cruel accident of fate. I can laugh off fate. It's a deliberately stupid choice."

"I'm glad you feel that way," Jane said, "because I want to talk about April."

"You didn't invite me over to discuss taxes, did you?" Shelley asked, frowning.

"No! I'd never talk to you about anything to do with

the I.R.S. It makes the veins in your forehead bulge, which isn't pretty. So, do you know Livvy Thatcher?"

"Not if I fell over her. Any relation to Margaret?"

Jane poured Shelley a big mug of hot coffee and led the way to the living room where piles of magazines and library books were stacked all over the floor. "Not so you'd notice."

"Good Lord, Jane, it looks like your bookshelves exploded! What *is* all this stuff? Wedding magazines? You didn't suddenly change your mind about marrying Mel, did you?"

"Nope, we agreed we're better off not even living together. This is to do with Livvy Thatcher. She was at the neighborhood Christmas cookie exchange I had here last month. Another neighbor dragged her along."

"Youngish? Tall? Bland-looking but awfully well made up?" Shelley asked, pulling up her mental inventory of the guests.

"Right. She called me yesterday. Asked if she could drop by and talk something over with me. I was afraid she was going to try to sell me something, to tell the truth, but I let her come over anyway. Chalk it up to January boredom."

"So what did she sell you?"

"Nothing. She said she'd been really impressed with my party. How well-planned and pleasant it was and how I managed to carry it off during a busy season without looking frazzled."

"She didn't say that. You're just bragging," Shelley said, flipping through a magazine and making a moue of distaste over a particularly ugly gown.

"She did, too. Word for word. Cross my heart. Then

she told me that she's getting married in April and wants me to help her plan the wedding."

Shelley glanced up. "You? Plan a wedding? What do you know about weddings?"

"I had one of my own once, you know. That's how I ended up with three kids."

"But you didn't even plan that one, I'll bet. The wedding, not the kids. Your mother did. Right?"

"Yes, but I was *there,*" Jane said.

"Jane, a wedding is a huge headache. Why would you help with one for a perfect stranger?"

"Money," Jane said. "And to see if I can."

"She's paying you?"

"Lots," Jane said, rubbing her hands together.

"You don't need money," Shelley persisted.

"I don't *desperately* need money, but it can't hurt. Another mysterious piece of machinery fell out of the bottom of my station wagon yesterday. I'm going to have to replace it soon."

"I really can't believe you're seriously considering it."

"I am. The week after New Year's kind of got to me," Jane admitted.

"How so?"

"After two weeks of being exhaustingly busy, I took down the decorations, the kids went back to school, and after sleeping it all off, I was so bored that I actually contemplated cleaning the basement."

"That's scary!" Shelley said.

"I've got one kid in college. Two of them will be home by four o'clock. But in another year and a half, only one will be home. And a couple years after that, none will be here every day."

"So marry Mel then," Shelley said. "Or work on that endless book you're writing."

"I hope you're just playing devil's advocate," Jane said.

"Hmmm. I guess I am," Shelley admitted. "I've given the same thing some serious thought from time to time lately. But planning a wedding! Ye gods, Jane. I wonder if you've ever really been around a bride."

"Oh, yes. A few relatives. And some of them got pretty nutsy. But this is different. Livvy's one of those overachieving yuppies. She pretty much runs her father's business and just wants a fabulous wedding—only because it's a social requirement—without the bother of making a lot of decisions and having her time taken up."

"You're sure she means that?"

"I am. She gave me the name of a caterer, a seamstress, and a florist she likes and said everything else is up to me. She'll supply the guest list, the china and silver patterns she likes, and will pick the day. There isn't even going to be a hassle over renting space because she's having the whole thing at some sort of hunting lodge that belongs to the family."

"A wedding at a hunting lodge?" Shelley yelped with laughter. "I love it. Bridesmaids in fluorescent orange. Gun racks for wedding gifts. Do you suppose the groom will wear one of those checkered hats with the earflaps?"

Jane bridled. "I think it's a very nice hunting lodge. Livvy told me it used to be a monastery."

Shelley slapped both hands over her mouth to stifle a shriek of glee. "Oh, it's too good to be true!" she said when she finally got herself under control.

"So you agree it's a good idea?"

"It's a bizarre idea, Jane. A wedding in a monastery-turned-hunt-club. But too much fun to resist. I capitulate. I endorse this heartily. You go, girlfriend."

"And you'll help me, right?" Jane asked.

Shelley instantly stopped laughing.

Chapter 1

April

It was very early in the morning, but the station wagon was loaded to the gunwales. Jane had all her notebooks full of lists, and a suitcase full of clothes for the couple days she'd be at "command central," a.k.a. the hunting lodge né monastery. She double-checked her notebooks while Shelley stumbled about sleepily putting her few belongings in the car. It was only about an hour and a half drive, but Jane didn't want to have to waste time coming home for anything she'd forgotten.

"I still don't quite understand why we have to go up there a couple days early," Shelley said with a fairly ladylike yawn.

"Because there's a lot to do on site," Jane answered.

" 'On site.' My, that sounds professional," Shelley commented. "I have to admit you've been pretty cool about this whole thing. I expected a lot more whining."

"I don't whine," Jane said. "Well, not as often as I might. It's just a matter of being really organized. I appreciate your coming along to help out at the end though."

"So what's the plan?" Shelley asked as they buckled their seat belts and Jane handed her a map. Shelley held it out in front of her at a significant distance. Jane considered opening a discussion about bifocals, but decided it wouldn't be politic when Shelley was being helpful.

"Today we just look everything over," Jane said. "I've got a rough sketch of the house plan, but I've never actually been there. I drove out there last week, but couldn't get the guy who lives there to come to the door. I should have called ahead."

"Somebody lives in this place?"

"A man Livvy calls 'Uncle Joe.' A family retainer who takes care of the building and grounds. For the time being, at least. The place is scheduled to be torn down this summer to put in a country club. Let's see—what else is happening today? The caterer is coming to look over the kitchens and move in his own cooking paraphernalia and the food, and the florist is also coming out today to figure out where to put all the arrangements. Then there's the seamstress." Jane waved good-bye to her mother-in-law, who was staying with the children while Jane was gone, and pulled out into the street.

"The seamstress is coming early?"

"Well, that's the only problem I foresee," Jane admitted. "You see, the bridesmaids' dresses aren't done yet. I've nagged and nagged and she keeps assuring me they'll be finished, but I have my doubts. So I insisted that she bring her sewing machine up to the lodge to finish them so I can stand right over her and keep on nagging."

"And maybe have to finish the dresses yourself?" Shelley said. Then her eyes widened. "Oh! You think *I'll* finish them!"

"It had crossed my mind," Jane said, grinning. "You're awfully good at sewing. Much better than I am."

"Jane, you know I don't sew! When have you ever seen me with a needle and thread in hand?"

"But you're so good at everything," Jane said with gooey sweetness.

Shelley snorted. "You don't have to bribe me with false flattery. I'm already in this with you. So what did the place look like? I'm a bit wary of lodges of any sort."

That was understandable. The previous fall, Shelley and Jane had been part of a committee investigating a resort facility that had put in a bid to provide a camping experience for their local high school. The weekend had quite incidentally included a double murder and the two women had spent a number of harrowing hours in the main lodge of the resort.

"Nothing like the Titus place," Jane assured her. "It just looks like a monastery that was turned into a hunting lodge. Really big. Old. Sprawling every which way. Additions that look like they might peel off the main building any second. The Thatchers must be very fond of the place to want to have a wedding there."

"I thought you just said they were letting it be torn down."

Jane nodded. "Fond enough, at least, to have one last big party there before making a killing on the country club deal."

After an hour, they stopped at what they judged to be the last outpost of civilization that served breakfast and Shelley asked, "Has the seamstress finished the wedding dress?"

"Oh, yes. And it's beautiful. Mrs. Crossthwait is a very

difficult woman, but her work is fantastic. It's just the bridesmaids who might have to wear pattern pieces and swatches. They all agreed to come today for their final fittings."

"What are their dresses like?"

"All different. I picked a cherry pink slubbed silk and let them each choose whatever kind of dress suited them."

"Jane! What a good idea. Bridesmaid dresses usually are to the taste of the bride, not the wearer, and hang around useless in closets the rest of their lives. I still have the revolting yellow pinafore thingie I had to wear in a cousin's wedding just because I can't stand to get rid of something I've only worn once. Can you picture me in a pinafore-style dress?"

Jane laughed at the image. "I understand these girls—there are three of them—are very different shapes and sizes. One is wearing a little slip dress with a matching shawl scarf. The plump one picked a boxy jacket and A-line skirt and the third is froufrou. Sort of 'plantation prom,' from the looks of the pattern. But at least they'll all have the same color and fabric. And the bride is carrying a bouquet of matching pink tulips."

"Jane, I hate to admit it, but I'm really impressed. You figured this all out yourself?"

"I'm not a complete cretin. And it's fun when somebody else is not only paying for it all, but paying me as well."

"What are these girls like?" Shelley asked.

"I've never met them. I just sent them samples of the fabric, told them to choose a style and go to the seamstress. It was a breeze . . . until I called each of them last week to see how their dresses had turned out and realized Mrs.

Crossthwait was falling behind in her sewing. I think we're almost there. Check the map."

There was a split rail fence running along the right side of the road with heavy woods behind it. The turn into the drive was unmarked and almost invisible. The long drive twisted and turned through the woods and emerged at the erstwhile monastery. It was an old unadorned clapboard building, suiting the simplicity of the religious order by whom it had been originally constructed. It had a vaguely barn-like look due to the scarce and small windows on the first floor, but the second floor, while obviously old as well, was clearly an addition. It had a steep roof with scattered dormers. There was a long wing to the left of the two-story section. It, too, looked like the ground floor was original and the upper story was an addition. The structure had a number of outbuildings and additions as well.

"It's not where I'd pick to get married," Shelley said. "What would you call this style? Midwestern wooden Gothic?"

"It looks vaguely Russian to me," Jane said. "All it's lacking is the onion dome."

As she spoke, an old man came shuffling around the corner of the house, stopped abruptly, and eyed them with suspicion. Jane hopped out of the car and approached him. "You must be Joe," she said, feeling the honorific "Uncle" was inappropriate and having no idea what his surname might be.

"That's right, missy," he growled. "And who might you be?"

"I'm Jane Jeffry. The wedding planner. I wrote you that my friend and I would be here today."

He scratched his head. "Yeah, I reckon you did. I got

everything ready for the big day. Had the plumbing looked over and took all the covers off the furniture like Livvy told me to."

Like many old men, he'd lost any sense of pattern he might have ever possessed. His trousers were a faded, but formerly colorful polyester checked pattern, his flannel shirt was brown plaid, and his jacket was a dark striped item that reminded Jane of old-fashioned prison garb. This was topped off by a thatch of wild white hair, a grizzly two-day growth of beard, and a fierce scowl.

"Could you show us around?" Jane asked, before introducing Shelley, who had joined them.

He gave a curt nod. "This here's the house proper. Reckon that's all you need to see." He opened the heavy front door and shuffled inside, leaving them to follow. The door caught Shelley on the elbow on the back swing and she uttered a very rude remark. There was a dark entry hall with a lot of doors opening to heaven knew what rooms.

Uncle Joe opened one and said, "Here's the main room where I reckon they'll have the wedding."

It was vast and dark. A huge chandelier that appeared to be made of antlers and fitted out with 25-watt light bulbs cast a faint glow. There were two fireplaces, one at each side of the room, and a good deal of substantial old furniture grouped around each. At the far end, there was an impressive staircase with a large landing at the top.

"Good grief!" Shelley said quietly, goggling at the furniture. "Do you know what this stuff goes for in the antique market? A fortune!"

"Shelley, brace yourself," Jane whispered back. "Look at the walls."

Shelley glanced around, inhaling with a gasp. There

was a virtual herd of mounted dead animal heads. Mostly deer, but a few elk, a matched set of moose heads, and one enormous buffalo taking pride of place above one of the fireplaces. She gaped for a moment, then said, "Well . . . you did say it was a hunting lodge, but I never imagined . . ."

Uncle Joe had disappeared into the gloom. They heard the faint sound of a door opening somewhere.

Jane said, "I guess we're on our own to explore further. It looks fairly clean in here, don't you think?"

"It's so dark it's impossible to tell. What are you doing about seating for the ceremony?"

Jane peered toward the far end of the room. "That's a nice wide staircase down there, isn't it? Livvy can come down that way—it would really show off her dress and we can shove the furniture that's here back against the walls farther. I have a company bringing in and setting up very nice folding chairs the morning of the wedding."

"Is this room, huge as it is, going to hold everybody?" Shelley asked.

Jane sat down on a big leather sofa that enveloped her like a grandmother's hug, and said, "That's the odd thing, Shelley. There aren't that many guests. I only sent out seventy-five invitations and a great many of them were out-of-towners who sent gifts but aren't coming. Business associates, I assume. There are only about forty people coming—plus the staff that will be staying here. You, me, the seamstress, caterer, and florist. And the immediate family members, of course."

"Don't forget Uncle Joe," Shelley said. "Doesn't it seem a bit odd to go to such trouble and expense for such a small wedding?"

"It's what Livvy wanted," Jane said. "Who am I to argue with a bride?"

"Where are the rest of the guests staying?"

"There's a smallish motel quite close. I've reserved the whole place. And most of the family will stay here. Let's look at the bedrooms. If we can find them."

They groped their way through the big main room, and found a passageway opening off the left side. Along it were twelve tiny rooms on each side of a long hallway. "These must have been the monks' rooms," Shelley said, opening the closest door with considerable trepidation.

It was a very small room with a single bed, a nightstand with a kerosene lamp, a wardrobe closet, and a chair and small rickety table by the window, which was square, but hardly larger than a porthole. The furniture was old, solid, and plain. The bed had a rather flat pillow and a noticeably dusty quilt on it. Its colors were drab; it was the sort of quilt people used to make out of old dress suits. A second door led to a bathroom the same size as the bedroom, which had ugly, but clean, workable fixtures that looked as though they'd been installed in the 1950s. It had slightly peeling wallpaper with faded roses and a pink linoleum floor. The opposite door in the bath led to another identical bedroom.

Shelley stepped out into the hall and opened a few other doors and came back. "They're all exactly the same," she said. "I'll bet these were the monks' rooms and one out of every three was turned into a bathroom."

"They're certainly . . ." Jane sought the right word. ". . . serviceable."

"It was meant for hunters, Jane, and whatever few misguided wives who might occasionally come along. It's a 'guy' place. They'd go out killing things all day, come back, and eat and drink all evening and tell fabulous stories of the woolly mammoth that got away, then fall into bed half-soused. A great-uncle of mine had a place like this when I was a kid. Not as big as this, but pretty much the same. My dad took me on one of the hunting trips when I was about seven. I had to sit around with my dad and uncles in a cold, wet duck blind all day. Worst trip of my life, but the men seemed to love it."

"I want to make a quick sketch of the rooms and assign them to the people who are staying here instead of the motel. Then let's go see what's upstairs," Jane said.

"Ghosts of monks, I'll bet," Shelley said cheerfully.

Jane glared at her. "If you try to tell me a ghost story in this spooky old place, I'll go home and stick you with the job of putting on this wedding!"

Chapter 2

When they explored the upstairs, they discovered that the area over the main room on the ground floor had been divided into three good-sized bedrooms. Two were merely larger versions of the monks' cells. But one of them, presumably that of the original Thatcher, was more furnished—not better furnished, just more. There were hunting prints and more animal heads on the walls and a large, molting bearskin rug on the floor next to the double bed. There were also two leather easy chairs and a desk that sat before a large window with a wonderful view out over the woods.

"I guess I'll put Livvy in here since the bride should have the best room," Jane said, "and move Dwayne in after the wedding. I'll put Mrs. Crossthwait in the middle one so she has plenty of room for her sewing and fittings. She's deaf enough that she won't be offended by sleeping next door to newlyweds. And I'll put Livvy's father at the far end, since he's the Big Cheese who's paying for everything. The other relatives and the bridal party can stay in the broom-closet-sized rooms."

"I wonder where that dear Uncle Joe lives?" Shelley said.

"Probably in a cave somewhere," Jane said. "I was hoping he'd be enthusiastic, maybe even have the urge to be helpful. He is, after all, employed by the father of the bride and apparently has nothing to do most of the time."

"Then you'll have to just insist that he make himself useful," Shelley said. "What's over the monks' rooms?"

They crossed the landing at the top of the stairs and found a room that was a gigantic attic. It had a long row of dormers along the front side, so it could have been made into more sleeping quarters, but apparently there had been no need and it had become the catchall. There was a whole floor down, but nothing but the studs on the walls.

There were old hunting rifles, heavy wool jackets, a box full of warm hats, some traps, hardware, cleaning utensils—all of this visible from the doorway. Jane could only guess what else was stashed here. At least most of the stuff was along the walls and there was an aisle through the middle. Someone had once put down a pretty rag rug near the doorway, but the colors were dulled by a long accumulation of dust.

"We ought to take those quilts downstairs outside to shake and air," Shelley said. "Maybe we could persuade Joe to string up a clothesline somewhere."

Jane went out to the landing and bellowed, "Joe! Joe! Where are you? We need some help here."

There was no reply, so she kept shouting periodically as she and Shelley made their way back to the small guest rooms. When they took the first quilt off the bed, they realized there was no other bedding. No sheets or pillow-cases. Jane stared at the naked mattress. "Oh, no! Now what do we do? There must be linens somewhere."

Shelley went to the door and shouted for Joe, and jumped when he appeared in the doorway of the next room. "I ain't deaf, lady."

Shelley considered asking him what he was doing eavesdropping on them from the next room in that case, but instead said mildly, "Where are the linens for the beds?"

"I sent 'em all out to the laundry last week. Ought to be back today."

Jane nearly collapsed in relief. She'd had visions of ransacking the countryside for an ungodly number of sets of sheets and pillowcases. "I'd like for you to rig up a clothes-line and put these quilts out to air, please," she said. The "please" was only a nicety. She'd hoped the request sounded more like an order.

"Gonna rain," he said.

"If and when it does, you can bring them back in." Jane was starting to get a little testy. Livvy had led her to believe that Uncle Joe, while a bit crusty, was something of a workhorse around the place, which obviously wasn't true. "There's a car pulling up outside. I hope it's Mrs. Crossthwait."

And so it turned out to be. She drove, somewhat surprisingly, a very sporty Jeep which was full of sewing paraphernalia. Her sewing machine, an ironing board, various ironing objects that Jane believed were called "hams," boxes of thread and fabric, pins and bias tape, envelopes full of tissue pattern pieces, and a lot of assorted items Jane couldn't begin to identify. There was also the enormous box containing the wedding dress and three smaller boxes housing the partially completed bridesmaids' apparel. "I'm so glad you're here, Mrs. Crossthwait!" Jane said.

"What's that, dear?"

Jane repeated herself, shouting a bit. "We'll help you get this all to your room. I'll have the handyman take your sewing machine when he finishes another job."

Mrs. Crossthwait was one of those people with round, plump faces that didn't quite match her tiny little body. Her hands were big-knuckled but still agile and she appeared to be bustling even when standing perfectly still. She flung up the back door of the vehicle and started loading Jane and Shelley down with boxes and small cases of tools and materials.

"I don't like the looks of this place," Mrs. Crossthwait said.

"I'm sorry about that," Jane said. "But we've given you an excellent room to work in. Lots of light and space and a good sturdy sewing table right by a window."

They started toward the house. "It's not that," Mrs. Crossthwait said. "It's a bad place. A bad aura. Wicked things have happened here and will happen again."

Shelley's intolerance of auras amounted to near obsession.

"Well, it better happen pretty soon because the house is being torn down in a couple months," she said briskly. "Come along, Mrs. Crossthwait. I'm so eager to see the dresses."

"Nice enough girls they are, the bridesmaids," Mrs. Crossthwait mumbled, puffing as she tried to keep up with the younger women. "Hope nothing happens to them."

Jane turned to roll her eyes at Shelley, missed her footing on the surprisingly slick steps, and nearly dropped a whole case of bobbins.

They got Mrs. Crossthwait settled in the upstairs room, which turned out to be something of a mistake because she climbed the stairs so slowly and awkwardly. Jane and Shelley made three trips with sewing materials in the time it took Mrs. Crossthwait to ascend the stairs. Then they went looking for Uncle Joe. He'd strung a grungy old rope between a couple trees and was just trying to make his escape when they caught up with him. "We need you to take the seamstress's sewing machine to her. It's in the Jeep in front and she's in the middle bedroom upstairs," Jane said.

"Sorry, miss. Bad back."

"Then you can use that dolly I saw in the attic," Jane insisted.

He muttered something that might have been an obscenity and shuffled off.

Jane and Shelley started hauling quilts outside. The laundry truck arrived just as they brought out the first four quilts. The driver of the white van hopped down and started setting white butcher-paper-wrapped parcels on the steps. "This is the Thatcher place, right?" he asked.

Jane confirmed that it was.

"Did you know these are linen sheets? We had to charge extra."

"Linen sheets?" Shelley asked. "The real things?"

"Genuine antiques," the deliveryman said.

Jane ran and got the checkbook Livvy had set up to pay for wedding expenses. As the truck pulled away, Shelley said, "Somebody has or had a *lot* of money. I wonder what's going to happen to the linens when the house is torn down."

"I imagine they'll get an antiques dealer in before then," Jane said.

"I wouldn't mind having some of those sheets," Shelley said, having opened one of the packages. She was greedily stroking a soft linen pillowcase.

Another vehicle was coming up the drive. This, too, was a closed white van, but was painted along the sides with a colorful garland of flowers. A willowy young man with shoulder-length blond hair, perfectly faded jeans, and a violently vivid Hawaiian shirt hopped out and strode toward Jane, his arms outstretched. "My darling Jane, I have finally arrived. Traffic was positively deadly, but I persevered for your sake." He folded her in a careful embrace.

Once Jane was released, she said, "Shelley, this is Larkspur. Larkspur, Shelley Nowack—my best friend who's helping me pull this wedding off."

"You've mentioned her. I'm charmed to meet you, Shelley. What wonderfully Pre-Raphaelite cheekbones you have, my dear."

Shelley touched her face. "Oh . . . have I really?"

"Divine. If I were a painter, I'd paint you," he proclaimed. "I must see the gardens first."

"I don't think there are any," Jane said, glancing around.

"The ghosts of gardens, I should have said," Larkspur explained. "I saw the tiniest glimpse of a bleeding heart right over there and where there's bleeding heart, there has been a garden. The old heirloom plants are so much better than some of the new varieties, don't you think? I wouldn't think anyone would mind if I just dug up a few little plants, would they?"

"I'm sure it would be fine," Jane said. "It's doomed to become a golf club this year anyway."

He threw his hands in the air dramatically. *"Horrors!* Horrible old men in light blue polyester pants traipsing around acres of boring grass. Then I must rescue some of the abandoned darlings that have survived the neglect. It's a sacred duty. And maybe I'll find time to search for the secret treasure as well." He laughed merrily.

"Secret treasure?" Jane asked.

"You don't *know* the story?" he trilled. "Then I shall have to tell you all about it, but I must explore the gardens first and see what poor, neglected plants are here." He wandered off, making happy little exclamations to himself.

"Is he Larkspur Smith or Bob Larkspur?" Shelley said, smiling.

"I have no idea. He refuses to be called anything but Larkspur. It takes a little getting used to."

"I wonder what Pre-Raphaelite cheekbones are," Shelley mused.

"I don't know, but you've got a couple of them, it seems."

They hung the first quilts. "We need one of those old-fashioned tennis racket-like things to knock the dust off," Shelley said.

"A carpet smacker?"

"I'm sure that's not the technical term, but I know what you mean," Shelley said. "Another arrival."

A rather old red compact car came up the drive and a

young woman got out. "Is one of you ladies Mrs. Jeffry?" she asked in a soft voice. She was lovely—with a slim body, long legs, and a mass of dark hair pulled into a ponytail. She was dark-skinned. Perhaps part Indian or Spanish, Jane thought, but had startlingly blue eyes. She was wearing jeans and a white shirt with the tails tied at her waist.

"I'm Jane, and you have to be Layla Shelton," Jane said.

"How could you know?" the young woman said with a smile.

"I've seen your dress. It couldn't possibly fit anyone else. It's done, except for the fringe on the shawl. Don't worry. I have Mrs. Crossthwait here under lock and key to make sure they get done in time."

"Are you sure? I felt bad when you called and I tattled that she didn't seem to be getting along very quickly."

"I'm glad you did tattle. We'll have everything done in time," Jane said, hoping she wouldn't have to eat her words. She introduced Shelley and then said, "There's supposed to be a handyman to help with your bags, but I think he's run away from home."

"I don't need help," Layla said. "But it looks like you might. You're airing those quilts?"

"We're just going in for the next batch," Jane said.

Layla came along, seemingly eager to help. "I hope you don't mind that I'm very early," she said. "I don't suppose Livvy's even here yet. But with two children to escape from, a smart woman gets while the getting is good. I'll probably miss them by this evening, but the prospect of freedom went to my head."

They discussed Layla's children while putting the freshly cleaned linens on the first four beds. They were four-year-old twins, a boy and girl, and Jane and Shelley were amazed to learn their total birth weight was over thirteen pounds. Layla's waist nipped in and her stomach was as flat as a breadboard. Further proof that Life Isn't Fair.

"Have you known Livvy long?" Shelley asked.

"In a way. We were friends in high school, and kept in touch during college, but I hadn't heard from her in a good seven years until she called and asked me if I'd be her bridesmaid. I was surprised, but so eager to have a little vacation from my family that I accepted."

"Maybe she just wanted to renew the friendship," Jane said. "You both live in the Chicago area."

"Oh, yes. But I haven't heard from her again since she called."

"That's very odd, isn't it?" Shelley asked, expertly making a hospital corner with a sheet.

"It would be odd for me, but not so much so for Livvy. She's always been dead set on being a good businesswoman and never socialized much. I don't even remember her having a single date in high school. She was always studying."

"What business is she in?" Shelley asked.

"Her family's, I imagine," Layla said. "At least that was her aim then. She's an only child whose mother died when she was very young. She used to be determined to be both daughter and son to her father. I never met him and she never said anything outright, but I got the impression he was very demanding and never quite let her forget that she was a mere girl, something of a disappointment."

Jane nodded. "I've only met with her four or five times to work out wedding details, and I never asked about her personal life, but I can well imagine that what you say of her is still true. She's remarkably bland and self-controlled. Almost entirely detached from the wedding planning, really. And the only suggestions I made that were rejected were because 'Daddy wouldn't like that.' In fact, her wedding dress is a very simple style because Daddy doesn't like ruffles and lace."

"I wonder if Daddy likes the groom?" Shelley said.

Jane shrugged. "I've never met either Dad or the groom."

"Then you're not a relative?" Layla asked.

"I'm hardly even an acquaintance," Jane admitted. "She just hired me to take care of all the details. She mentioned having a couple of aunts, but when I asked why they weren't helping her, she just said they weren't suitable." Actually, Livvy had said they were a couple of old bats, but it didn't seem tactful to repeat the exact wording.

Shelley cocked an eyebrow. "Unsuitable aunts? That's a bit scary. Say, Layla, the florist mentioned something about a treasure here. Do you know what he meant?"

"A treasure? No, I don't— Oh, maybe I do. Let me think. I believe her grandfather was extremely wealthy. This was his place, you know. A bunch of us were invited here once in high school for a dance not long after the grandfather had died and somebody asked her about a treasure. Livvy pooh-poohed the idea. Apparently he hadn't left as much money as her aunts expected and they'd been telling people he'd hidden the rest of his fortune somewhere." Layla took another sheet out of its packaging and snapped it open. "At least, I think that was the gist of it. I only remember that much because I was sixteen and this seemed the kind of spooky place where there might be a hidden treasure. I guess I'd read too much Nancy Drew as a child."

They finished making the bed and Layla added, "Oh, I know who could tell you about it. Livvy's father and his best friend and hunting buddy both had daughters the same age. I can't remember her name at the moment, but Mrs. Crossthwait mentioned her as being one of the other bridesmaids. Mrs. C. was complaining about all the fancy stuff on the dress."

"Oh, that's Eden Matthews," Jane said.

"That's right," Layla replied. "Livvy sometimes whined about having to spend so much time with Eden because their dads were friends. Eden is a bit on the earthy side, I assume."

"She complained about her and still picked her as a bridesmaid?" Jane asked.

Layla laughed. "My bet is that she was another decision that Daddy made."

Shelley fluffed up one of the limp pillows and stuffed it into a pillowcase. "Why do I have the feeling that we're not all going to be real crazy about Daddy?"

Chapter 3

Mr. Willis, the caterer, arrived just before noon. Jane had begun to teeter on the brink of panic again because there was hardly a scrap of food in the house and she had no idea where to even find burgers and fries for Mrs. Crossthwait, Layla, Larkspur, Shelley, and herself. Uncle Joe, wherever he'd taken refuge, certainly had food and probably wouldn't have shared it even if they'd begged for crusts.

Mr. Willis was a tubby little man with a big round head like a pumpkin, perched on top of which was a tottering chef's hat. Jane wondered if he didn't have to glue it to his sparse fair hair to keep it in place. He was probably only in his late twenties, but was stuffy and formal enough to have been much older. He had a spotty teenaged girl assistant who looked like she could step right into the role of Victorian skivvy. He didn't bother to introduce her.

"This kitchen," he exclaimed, investigating his domain, "is a disgrace."

"I did warn you that it might be," Jane said rather than argue with him.

Actually, the kitchen was the only place Uncle Joe seemed to have done much to. The old-fashioned six-burner gas stove was reasonably clean; the big double ovens were ancient, but had only a dusting of crumbs on the bottom. The refrigerator, which was empty except for a loaf of bread and a bottle of milk, was huge and old enough to qualify as an antique. There was also a smallish, more modern freezer, entirely empty, but recently defrosted. There was a very unattractive brown and cream linoleum floor, but the big, deep sinks almost made up for it. Except for a coffeemaker, there were no modern appliances, but Mr. Willis had brought his own favorite gadgets anyway.

The skivvy dragged in a Cuisinart, a blender, a box full of very expensive-looking utensils and truly wicked knives. Then she went back for pots and pans, some of which Jane guessed were worth a good deal more than most large pieces of furniture.

"What about dishes?" Mr. Willis asked, impervious to the skivvy's puffing and panting.

Jane opened a series of cabinets across the room. The house had been built for entertaining and feeding vast numbers and there was a generous and surprisingly high-quality selection of plates, bowls, silverware, and glasses. She had expected Mr. Willis to be impressed, but he just sniffed, "They'll all have to be washed."

"I suppose they will," Jane said mildly and thought, *If you think I'm doing it, you're doomed to disappointment.*

The skivvy was now hauling in food in grocery bags

and coolers while Mr. Willis gazed about disapprovingly. Jane noticed a neat pile of *Field and Stream* magazines stacked in the pantry and an ashtray with what looked like a fairly fresh cigar stub in it. The kitchen, she figured, was probably Uncle Joe's favorite room.

Jane and Shelley made their escape as quickly as possible. Layla was sitting in the main room, idly flipping through a magazine. "It's so quiet here," she said, smiling. "No children. Do you suppose there's a jigsaw puzzle somewhere?"

"I wouldn't be surprised," Jane said. "This place was meant for leisure activities." With a little searching, they found a cabinet full of entertaining items. Jigsaw puzzles in abundance, packs of playing cards, board games, checker and chess sets. Even a Ouija board. They'd have to make sure Mrs. Crossthwait didn't learn about that and go off on auras again.

"I'm so glad I had to come early for my last dress fitting," Layla said. "I can hardly remember the last time I had Nothing To Do. I'm loving it."

"Have you had the fitting?" Jane asked. "Is your dress nearly ready?"

"Yes. Mrs. Crossthwait is buzzing away up there on her sewing machine. She's a bit short on the social graces, isn't she? Jumped all over me for having the wrong shoes and underwear and then went off on a tangent about being careful of bad auras."

There was a sudden loud "Bong!" which startled all of them.

"What was that?" Layla asked.

"Either the doorbell, or someone announcing the end of the world," Shelley said.

The woman at the door was not so much overweight as stocky. Short, but with a big-boned look. With that figure and the oddly crimped short hair, she reminded Jane of the field hockey mistress at a school she'd attended in England when she was a teenager. "You must be Mrs. Jeffry," the young woman said. "I'm Kitty Wilson."

"Bring your things in, Kitty, and please call me Jane." Jane introduced her to Shelley and Layla and said, "I'll show you where your room is, then we better get you up to Mrs. Crossthwait for your last fitting."

"Are Livvy and Dwayne here yet?" Kitty asked as they made their way to the corridor with the monks' rooms.

"No, they don't arrive until tomorrow. There are lots of rooms, but they all share a bath with someone. I've put you and Layla together. Is that all right?"

"Oh, of course. Isn't Layla gorgeous? I wonder how Livvy knows her."

"They were in high school together. What's your connection to Livvy?"

"I'm a secretary at Novelties."

"Novelties?"

"The Thatcher family company. Livvy is vice president."

"I knew there was a family business," Jane said, "but I didn't know what it was. What does Novelties do?"

"We supply companies with personalized novelty items. Company t-shirts, mugs, pens, key chains, that sort of thing. With their company logo imprinted. We also make up award plaques and framed tributes to retiring employees. Most of the items are little junky things, but some are very nice. Expensive fountain pens with names in gold, crystal paperweights with carved accomplishments—fifty years' service awards and such."

"Here's your room. The bathroom is there and Layla's room is just beyond," Jane said. "What an interesting business. I never even wondered where all those things came from."

Kitty set her suitcases on the bed. She looked as if she'd packed for a month instead of just a couple days. Kitty had carried two big suitcases, Jane had carried a small one and a box. Jane half expected a trunk to be delivered later. "It's an old company," Kitty said. "Livvy's grandfather, Oliver Wendell Thatcher, founded it, I think. Or maybe it was his father. We have a little museum in the office complex with a bunch of old stuff they did. Wooden rulers with lumberyard names, stamped leather change purses from the twenties."

"This sounds like a big operation," Jane said. "And Livvy is vice president?"

"She's really the president and CEO although her father still officially holds those titles. But Livvy does all the work."

"And you're her secretary?"

"No, I'm the secretary of two of the sales reps. Oh, you're wondering, I imagine, why she chose me as a bridesmaid? That's because I introduced her to Dwayne. I had a blind date with him and we ran into Livvy at the movies. I introduced them and the rest, as they say, is history."

"Oh, I see. I'm sorry to rush you, but—"

"I know. The fitting."

Jane showed her to the big upstairs room where Mrs.

Crossthwait had been installed. Layla and Shelley were there as well, apparently out of sheer boredom. Kitty stripped down to her slip and tried on the jacket of her boxy suit. It was really enormously flattering to her chunky figure. Mrs. Crossthwait fussed about, measuring and turning the sleeves and pinning them in place.

"Is that all that remains to do?" Jane asked loudly.

"That and the skirt hem," Mrs. Crossthwait said. "Take off the jacket, dear."

Kitty slipped the skirt on and fumbled at the back of the skirt waistband for the button.

"I'll do that, dear," Mrs. Crossthwait said. "Hmmm. You've put on a bit of weight, haven't you?"

"I have not. You must have put the button in the wrong place." Kitty looked extremely embarrassed at having her figure criticized while she was standing around in her slip in front of strangers.

"I never mismeasure," Mrs. Crossthwait said firmly. "I'll have to let out a little of the ease and move the button."

Jane almost groaned out loud. More alterations. More delay.

"Shelley, could you help me make up the rest of the beds?" she asked.

"I'll help," Layla said.

"No, this smacks of housework. You're on vacation. Work on your jigsaw puzzle."

Jane was surprised and delighted to find that most of the little monk cells now had casual flower arrangements on the bedside tables. "I guess Larkspur has been busy," she said. "How pretty they are!"

"Did I hear my name being taken in vain?" Larkspur said from the doorway.

"These arrangements are marvelous. We hadn't talked about them in our planning, though."

He laughed. "If you're worried about your budget, don't. I found all the flowers in the woods and just stuck them in whatever containers your Mr. Willis would part with. No charge, Mrs. Midas. He's a bit of a dish, isn't he? The Willis."

"Is he cooking yet? I'm starved," Shelley said.

"Yes, in fact he sent me to find everyone. Lovely little cress sandwiches."

Lunch was elegant. They all gathered around the big, scarred kitchen worktable, although Mr. Willis wanted to serve them in the dining room. He was extremely unhappy to learn that there wasn't a dining room. "Where am I to serve the reception dinner then?" he asked.

"No problem," Jane assured him. "The rental people will set up the main room with rows of chairs, church-style with an aisle. As soon as the wedding is finished and pictures are being taken outside, they'll move the chairs back against the walls and put up the buffet table."

Larkspur was tapping his foot impatiently. "Oh, I'm not too fond of that plan. I'll have to be tearing about with the table flowers like a mad thing."

Jane said, "I'm sorry, but we have to work with the layout we've got. There's a smaller room just off the main room that probably once had a billiard table and we'll use that for the bridal shower tomorrow afternoon and the bachelor party later in the evening. You'll both be able to get in that room as early as you like to get set up. Meanwhile, we'll have to have our lunch today here in the kitchen."

Larkspur and Mr. Willis agreed, but grudgingly.

The skivvy served them. Mr. Willis ate his lunch silently, while double-checking the lists he'd made in a small notebook. Jane was doing the same with one of her notebooks. Shelley, Layla, and Kitty tried to find some common ground for conversation and Larkspur told Mrs. Crossthwait a string of arch little jokes. She stared at him as if he were from outer space, but probably harmless. "You're one of 'those' people, aren't you?" she finally said to Larkspur.

"Those people?"

"One of those pansy boys."

Larkspur's usual smile faded. "More of a sunflower, I'd have said," he snapped. And added, under his breath, "Dirty-minded old bat."

Halfway through the meal, Uncle Joe turned up, looking outraged at the invasion of his kitchen.

"We'd have invited you to lunch if we could have found you," Jane said sweetly. "Help yourself. Livvy's aunts will be arriving later this afternoon and we'll need you to carry bags. Please don't disappear again."

Uncle Joe just scowled at her.

When lunch was finished, everyone scattered. Jane sat down with her notebooks at the old-fashioned dial phone in the front hall. She called the local motel to confirm the rooms for the guests who wouldn't be staying at the house, checked that the rental people had the correct tables, chairs, and linens ready to go and had their directions for reaching the lodge right. She gave her mother-in-law a ring to make sure the kids were doing okay and got stuck hearing at length about how Willard, Jane's big, stupid, yellow dog, had brought a live (if only barely so) chipmunk into the house. The creature was still at large. Thelma speculated that it might be rabid. That it might bite her. That it might have babies somewhere in the house. Thelma tended toward dramatic speculations.

"Don't worry. The cats will find and dispatch it," Jane assured her. She didn't mention what sort of nasty messes this might involve. Thelma would find out soon enough.

Jane worked her way through the rest of her list, feeling very efficient and smug, then went to check on Mrs. Crossthwait's progress—which turned out to be nearly imperceptible. "I'm getting a little concerned," Jane said to the seamstress. "We're running out of time, you know."

Mrs. Crossthwait said, "Don't you worry, dear. The wedding is still two full days ahead. Plenty of time."

"But I don't want you to be sewing until the last second," Jane said. "I'd really like to have all the dresses done, pressed, and hung up for the girls by this evening."

"I'll have them done by noon tomorrow," Mrs. Crossthwait said, glaring. "I've been doing weddings since I was a slip of a girl and I know about deadlines. More than you do, I'd venture to say."

Jane suddenly felt an irrational wave of dislike for this woman. She was doing a meticulous job on the dresses, but couldn't she be a little less meticulous and get the damned dresses finished? Jane didn't want to be nagging the old woman, but everything else was so thoroughly under control and Mrs. Crossthwait was making Jane crazy with her dawdling and her outspoken rudeness to everyone.

"I plan to hold you to that promise," Jane said firmly.

But this turned out to be an empty threat. A very empty threat.

❖

Chapter 4

By mid-afternoon Jane was fretting about the third bridesmaid. She hadn't arrived and her dress was the most elaborate and farthest from completion. Jane was rummaging through her notebooks for Eden's telephone number when the young woman arrived.

"I hope you're Eden Matthews," Jane said to her. "I was about to set up a search party."

"And you must be Jane Jeffry. I'm sorry I'm late. Car problems," Eden said breezily. She dumped a large suitcase in the front hall, evidently certain that it would be handled from here on by someone else. "The old lodge never changes," she said, strolling into the main room. "I'm going to hate seeing this old place torn down. I've spent a good deal of time here over the years."

"You're an old friend of Livvy's, aren't you?" Jane said.

Eden made a "so-so" motion with her hand. "We've known each other all our lives," she said. "Our fathers are best friends and business associates. Ah, this is the best chair in the place," she said, flopping down on a deep leather armchair.

Jane was surprised at Eden's appearance. They'd never met before, only talked on the phone, but Eden had a very soft voice and Jane had formed a totally unfounded impression that Eden was small and meek. But she was a tall, well-rounded glamour girl—reminiscent of a young Farah Fawcett, but with a voluptuous figure. Lots of artfully tousled hair, stunning teeth, perfect skin, and a runway model's walk.

The bridesmaid dress she'd chosen—a mass of draped ruffles cascading down from a deep neckline—now made sense. Tall, gorgeous, long-striding Eden was going to make poor Livvy look like Cinderella before the Fairy Godmother took her in hand. It was hard to outshine a bride, but Jane suspected Eden was going to do just that.

Jane was about to launch into a nag about dress fittings when Eden said, "So poor little Livvy really is going to marry Dwayne, the gas station attendant? She hasn't backed out yet?"

"Backed out! Not after all my work, she won't. The groom works at a gas station?" Jane asked.

Eden laughed softly. "No, he just looks like it. Sexy as hell, I have to admit, but greasy-looking. Like a gigolo at a cheap casino. But then"—she held up a finger and moved it back and forth like a metronome—"the clock is ticking. Livvy's nearly thirty and it's time to provide grandsons."

Jane sat down across from Eden. "You don't like her, do you?"

Eden looked shocked. "I *do* like Livvy. We grew up almost like sisters and you can't dislike a sister—"

Jane, who had a sister she wasn't crazy about, nearly objected to this premise.

"—but mostly I feel sorry for her," Eden went on.

"She's so vanilla custard, poor thing. So obedient. Jack Thatcher, her father, has thoroughly damped down any spirit or personality she might have had. She's spent her whole life trying to please him."

Eden stared at a moose head on the opposite wall and went on, more to herself than to Jane, "I remember when we were about seven years old. We came out here for the weekend and Livvy and I wandered off to play. We found some perfectly luscious mud and had a great time making absolute messes of ourselves. When we got back, Jack went ballistic. She'd ruined her dress, she was a mess, he was ashamed to have a daughter who could make such a pig of herself.

"Livvy cried for the entire weekend. I never saw her with so much as a smudge on her face or a wrinkle in her clothes again. And I never heard her laugh again, except politely."

"That's very sad," Jane said. "Does her father approve of Dwayne?"

"Good question. I don't suppose he cares much one way or the other. It's Livvy who has to live with him. Jack will probably just ignore him—as long as some handsome, healthy, intelligent grandsons come along pretty soon. And I'm sure Jack's arranged for a prenuptial agreement that would result in Dwayne standing in the cold in his Jockey shorts if the marriage doesn't work out or the grandsons don't appear promptly."

"Grandsons mean so much to him?"

"Oh, yes. Livvy is just the stopgap between him and the next generation of male Thatchers."

"Livvy's his only child, right?"

"Now she is. There was a son. A year or two older

than Livvy. The light of Jack's life, my dad said. But he died when Livvy was just a baby. Of mumps, of all things. And Jack, who hadn't had mumps as a child, got it too. My dad said Jack nearly went crazy when the little boy died and Jack realized he'd never be able to father a replacement."

"And Livvy's mother? What about her?" Jane asked.

"She was a nice woman, meek and pretty like Livvy. But she died of breast cancer when Livvy was about five. Poor Livvy. If she had to have a husband, I don't know why she couldn't have made a better choice."

"We don't always fall in love with the best choice," Jane said, thinking about her own ill-fated marriage.

"Love? I don't think it's love. It's necessity. As I say, the clock is ticking. Oh, dear, is that the aunties' shrill voices I hear?"

The voices in the front hall sounded a bit like outraged chickens squabbling over a choice piece of corn.

"Probably. They weren't supposed to come until tomorrow, but insisted on coming today." Jane and Eden got up and went to meet the newcomers.

The two tiny elderly ladies were virtually indistinguishable except for their hair. One had a snowy white do that towered over her like an impossibly fluffy cloud. The other had the identical style, but in a maroon red verging on purple that never grew from a human head. Jane wondered if they got a discount on the two dreadful wigs. They looked like something from a Disney cartoon.

"Auntie Iva," Eden said, bending down to hug the maroon one.

"Darling Eden," the old lady cooed. "You get taller every time I see you."

The white-wigged one was scrabbling at Eden's sleeve for her share of attention.

"Auntie Marguerite, you look divine," Eden said, and quickly added, "You both do."

Eden introduced them to Jane. "Miss Iva Thatcher, Mrs. Marguerite Rowe," she said quite formally, "this is Jane Jeffry, the lady who has put together Livvy's wedding."

The bright smiles with which they'd greeted Eden faded to scowls. "Yes, Mrs. Jeffry," Iva said coldly. "Livvy told us you were doing all the arrangements. We offered to plan the wedding ourselves. We are, after all, her aunts. Her only female relatives. The substitutes for her own dear, departed mother. But she preferred to have a complete stranger arrange the most important day of her life."

Before Jane could compose any reply, Eden jumped in. "But my dears, Livvy told me she wanted you two to be the guests of honor. You can't ask a guest of honor to do all the drudgery. Livvy wanted you to just sail in and thoroughly enjoy yourselves without having to fret over whether the flowers had arrived or the dresses fitted."

Eden turned and winked at Jane, but Jane didn't need the wink to know that Eden was lying through her spectacular teeth.

"Well, there is that aspect," Aunt Marguerite said. "It's so like Livvy to want to spare us trouble. Such a dear girl. And she's marrying such a handsome man."

"Get your mind out the gutter," Iva snapped.

Marguerite glowered. "Just because I'm not a dried-up spinster like some I could name—"

"I could have had as good a husband as you did, dear," Iva came back, "if I'd been foolish enough to believe that fake English accent and—"

"Now, my dears, let's don't have any tiffs," Eden said. Jane was surprised to learn that Eden could speak quite loudly when the occasion demanded it.

"Let me show you to your rooms," Jane said.

"Oh, we know where they are. Just up the stairs," Iva said.

"No, actually, those rooms are taken," Jane said, resisting the urge to wring her hands in despair.

"But we always stay in the big center room," Marguerite said.

"I had to put the seamstress in there so there would be room for her sewing," Jane explained.

"The seamstress is still sewing? Here?" Iva screeched. "Well, I can tell you if I'd been in charge, those dresses would have been done weeks ago. Still, we'll take one of the rooms next to it."

Jane sighed. She wasn't a confrontational person, but she was going to have to make clear just who *was* in charge or these ladies were going to run over her. They'd obviously spent decades practicing the art on each other.

"That's quite impossible," Jane said, looking Iva straight in the eye. "Livvy's father will be in one of the rooms. He is, after all, the owner of the house and the man who's paying for the wedding, and the bride gets the other one. I'll show you where you're staying."

They trailed along behind her, snipping at her and each other the whole way. When Jane returned to the main room, she found Shelley puttering around with a dust cloth. "I sent Eden up to the dressmaker. What a glamorous number she is," Shelley said. "You look frazzled."

"Wait until you meet the aunts," Jane said.

"They're here already?"

"Apparently they got in a dispute about starting early enough tomorrow and the one with a car insisted they come today instead. They're terrors. Shelley, we're surrounded by a bleating flock of cranky old ladies."

"You'll cope. And if you can't, I'll read them the riot act."

"I already coped. I was very firm with them. I'm turning into you."

"Then why don't you look more cheerful?" Shelley flicked the dust cloth over an old Victrola.

"I had an interesting chat with Eden," Jane said. "This family, it seems, is much stranger than I thought. And Eden doesn't seem to think Livvy's in love with Dwayne. Shelley, I'm horrified that I might have done all this work and the bride's going to bolt at the last minute."

"Do you really think so?" Shelley asked.

Jane repeated the gist of the conversation she'd had with Eden. "So she's just marrying to please her father with a mob of grandsons."

"According to Eden," Shelley reminded her. "But she may not be right. Livvy might be madly, passionately in love and is just too boring and repressed to show it. And even if she's not wild about him, she's getting a good-looking husband, a father for potential kids, and he's marrying into a lot of money. Marriages have been made for worse reasons and thrived."

Jane thought for a moment. "I never heard her say a warm word about Dwayne at our meetings. Of course, I never heard her express much of an opinion about anything. You're right. And it's not my problem. If she bolts, she bolts. Nobody can blame me. Though I'm sure the aunts will try to."

* * *

Jane let Mr. Willis know that there would be two more for dinner, then she and Shelley went in search of the missing members of the party. They found Larkspur digging around in an area next to an old well. "Finding anything?" Jane called to him.

He spun around so quickly he nearly toppled right in. "What a fright you gave me!" he said guiltily. "Just digging up some scilla bulbs that were planted around the well. I haven't seen them bloom, of course, and they might be utter duds—" He was babbling.

"You don't happen to know where Uncle Joe hides out, do you?" Jane asked, cutting him off as he launched into a description of the various hues of scilla.

"I *do* happen," Larkspur said. "There's a dreadful little house through the woods right there." He pointed toward an overgrown path. "It looks like a duck blind that took on a life of its own. I saw him leaving it and, I blush to admit, took the littlest peek through the window. He's made it quite comfy."

"Let's go roust him out," Shelley said.

They started off, and Jane turned back for a second. "Will you be here for dinner, Larkspur? If so, you need to tell Mr. Willis."

"I may stay," he said. "It looks like rain and I don't want to drive back in the dark in a nasty downpour. Yes, I'll stay over tonight and run back to the shop in the morning."

"He was blushing," Shelley said when they got into the woods. "I wonder why."

"And how did he happen to come prepared to stay overnight?" Jane asked.

Shelley smiled. "He planned to stay, didn't he? I think

he believes in this treasure story. Jane, did you see the size of the holes he'd dug around the well? Scillas are little bulbs that are just an inch or two under the surface. Larkspur was digging his way to China."

Jane laughed. "Just what I was thinking. But why the well?"

"If you were going to bury a treasure, you'd need to put it where you could easily find it again. Near a landmark that's going to be there for a good long time."

"We need to ask Eden about this treasure story," Jane said. "She's a good source of information."

Uncle Joe's hideout must have been a gamekeeper's cottage in a previous era. It was the lodge in miniature with the same well-weathered wooden clapboards, small windows, and a roof that had seen better days. Jane tapped on the door, waited a moment, then knocked more loudly. There was still no answer.

"Maybe he saw us coming," Shelley said.

"Do you suppose we could slip some sort of homing device on him?" Jane suggested as they started back to the lodge. "Or maybe put one of those invisible dog fences around the house and a collar on him?"

Shelley's reply was blotted out by a sudden, horrifying flash of lightning and a deafening blast of thunder.

They scurried like frightened rabbits and before they got safely inside, they were soaked with rain. By the time they'd changed clothes, there were a few shafts of sunshine and the rain was just a drizzle. Typical spring weather in the Midwest. Jane gazed out the tiny window of her little monk's cell room and could see the next lightning-flickering bank of black clouds coming in.

"It's going to be nasty," she called to Shelley, who was fluffing up her hair in the bathroom they shared.

"Good," Shelley answered. "It'll be fun. A big fire in that monster fireplace, the smell of kerosene lamps, Mr. Willis making cocoa in the kitchen, toasting marshmallows—"

"—singing camp songs?" Jane added. "Get a grip, Shelley. And keep in mind that if we lose power, Mrs. Crossthwait's sewing machine won't work and we'll have to pitch in and hand-sew in the dark."

Chapter **5**

Mr. Willis prepared a superb "country" dinner—a thick, rich beef stew with baby carrots, meat so tender it fell apart, and a broth so perfectly spiced it would have been delicious all by itself. There was also cornbread that Jane would swear for the rest of her life was the best she'd ever tasted. After baking it, Mr. Willis had cut squares, sliced them in half, slathered them with an herbed butter, and lightly broiled them. Mr. Willis wasn't afraid of cholesterol, it seemed.

Larkspur appeared for dinner in fresh clothes. Shelley and Jane exchanged knowing looks. He *had* come prepared to stay; the storm just gave him an acceptable excuse.

The aunties, Iva and Marguerite, had donned comfy jogging outfits that someone had ornamented with bits of lace. Iva's was a maroon that clashed horribly with her wig. Marguerite's was a powder blue that set off her pale eyes. Iva expressed a few lingering doubts about Jane having the privilege of planning the wedding, which Eden thoroughly squashed again. As Jane introduced Shelley to the aunts, she caught a glimpse of movement in the corner of her eye. Uncle Joe had turned up. The smell of dinner must have drawn him out of his lair.

He greeted Eden with rough affection. "It's that damned girl again! Can't stay away from here, can you?"

"Hello, you darling old geezer," Eden said, giving him a hug. She took charge of introducing him to the other bridesmaids, Kitty and Layla. He hardly glanced at Kitty, who looked especially clunky in baggy jeans and an oversized t-shirt, but he gazed as if mesmerized at Layla.

"Quit staring," Eden told him bluntly. "And say hello to Iva and Marguerite."

He nodded curtly. They barely looked up from their cornbread and stew to acknowledge his presence. Their disapproval of him couldn't be more obvious.

Mrs. Crossthwait was the last to arrive. She carefully avoided meeting Jane's questioning gaze.

"Are you making progress, Mrs. Crossthwait?" Jane asked.

"No, I've been taking a nap all afternoon," she snapped sarcastically. The "aura" of the place—or more likely Jane's nagging—was getting on her nerves. "Of *course* I'm making progress. You don't think I want these girls to wear dresses that aren't the best I can do, do you?" She smiled at Iva and Marguerite, her contemporaries, for approval. The aunts merely looked confused.

Jane sighed and let it go. She'd check after dinner on just how far along the seamstress was when the cranky old dear didn't have an audience for her complaints. The last thing she needed was *three* little old ladies talking her to bits.

Mrs. Crossthwait didn't approve of dinner. "It's too salty and I can tell you've used real butter," she accused.

"But of course I have," Mr. Willis said, drawing himself up to his full five feet four.

"Shouldn't a young man like you be more concerned with the health of the people he's feeding?"

"I wasn't aware I was going to be feeding *you*," Mr. Willis replied with an out-and-out sneer. Larkspur applauded the caterer's performance and the aunts glared at Jane as if this distasteful brouhaha were all her fault. The spotty skivvy cowered in the corner of the room like somebody from a Dickens novel.

It was all Jane could do to keep herself from banging her head on the table.

"Let's all play nice, darlings," Eden said.

Their dinner was interrupted several times by the lights flickering as the storm gathered force again. Mrs. Crossthwait screeched with alarm every time there was a clap of thunder. A gust of strong wind blew the front door open and Uncle Joe voluntarily went to close it, which was a surprise to Jane. It must have been to the aunts as well, as they whispered together when he'd left. After Mr. Willis had served strawberry shortcake with real whipped cream, which they all ate in spite of protestations about being too full to swallow another bite, the group started drifting away.

The three bridesmaids and Larkspur settled around a big table in the main room with a jigsaw puzzle and a very staticky radio to see if they could get a weather forecast. The aunts sat by the fireplace, whispering ferociously to each other.

"They're up to something, Jane," Shelley said.

"It sure looks like it. But what? They wouldn't sabotage Livvy's wedding just to spite me, would they?"

Uncle Joe, apparently feeling confident that Jane wasn't going to think of anything for him to do, stuck around for a while. He drifted toward the aunts, but didn't sit down with them. Instead, he sank into a chair nearby and made a big production of reading a newspaper. Lots of flapping of pages and intense scrutiny of newsprint to cover the fact that he, too, obviously wanted to know what kind of plot the aunts were hatching.

Jane let Mrs. Crossthwait off the hook for a bit. She could hardly rush her straight from dinner to work. She checked her watch and made a mental note to give the woman half an hour of leisure. Mrs. Crossthwait hovered around the jigsaw puzzle group. "Mrs. Jeffry probably won't agree, but there are good reasons for not finishing the dresses too far ahead," she said loudly enough to make sure Jane could hear her.

"Oh?" Eden said mildly, as she took a piece of the puzzle away from Larkspur and fitted it in place.

"How utterly clever you are," Larkspur said.

"Yes, people change," Mrs. Crossthwait said, not willing to let a general lack of interest from her audience keep her from explaining. "Kitty's gained weight since I did the cutting and Layla's lost a bit."

"I have *not* gained weight," Kitty said with her teeth gritted.

"And I'm afraid I haven't lost any," Layla said. "Anyway, the dresses are going to be just beautiful, I'm sure. Now, where are the sandy-colored pieces that are going to be the sidewalk part of the picture? Kitty, help me find all of them."

"What a lovely brush-off," Shelley whispered to Jane.

Mrs. Crossthwait recognized it as such and wandered aimlessly toward the aunts, thinking perhaps that she'd get a better reception from them. But this hope was dashed when they saw her coming and gave two cold, unblinking stares. Still, she persisted in asking if anyone had died here lately. She felt an aura of death.

"Certainly not!" Iva exclaimed, as though dying was a breech of good taste that couldn't happen to such as the Thatcher clan.

The seamstress dropped into the nearest chair to the aunts. "You don't seem to remember me," she said.

"Are you speaking to me?" Marguerite asked haughtily.

"I made your wedding dress."

"That was a long time ago and something I don't discuss with strangers," Marguerite said. She adjusted herself in her chair so that her back was to the seamstress, indicating quite clearly that the discussion had concluded.

Mrs. Crossthwait stared at Marguerite for a long moment, then pretended an interest in her surroundings for a few minutes longer, before getting up and trudging as slowly and carefully as a condemned prisoner up the stairs to her prison.

"I should feel sorry for her," Jane said quietly to Shelley. "That was a really formidable snub. But I'm too annoyed at her dawdling to feel any sympathy. She's being paid an absolute fortune to make the dresses. She's so damned annoying."

Within the hour, another storm front moved in with thunder that shook the house, made the radio squawk, and put the lights out for a few minutes. When they came back on, they were oddly dim for a while, then went out again.

"Phooey, I almost had the sidewalk finished," Layla said in the darkness.

"I think we might as well give it up for the night. It's almost nine-thirty anyway," Eden said. "I have a flashlight in my purse and I think we all have small kerosene lamps in our rooms. Anybody want to follow me? If we still don't have power tomorrow, we'll go into town and buy more flashlights."

The idea of the power being out for the wedding was something that had never crossed Jane's mind. How would Mr. Willis cook? How would Livvy see her way down the stairs? It would be like having the ceremony in a cave! She leaned over to Shelley. "Do you suppose there's a church anywhere near? I need to do some heavyweight praying."

Shelley just patted her hand.

"There's a town nearby?" Kitty asked.

"Well, sort of a town," Eden said. "A motel, Wanda's Bait and Party Shoppe, a bank, and a gun shop."

Kitty and Layla took her up on the offer to lead them into the darkness of the monks' cells hallway. The aunts had their own flashlight and followed along. Uncle Joe had disappeared into the darkness. Mr. Willis, still in the kitchen cleaning up from dinner, was cursing.

Shelley was doubled up in a chair, laughing herself silly about Wanda's Bait and Party Shoppe. "I love it! You can get your party accessories *and* your minnows without having to run all over town."

"My dears," Larkspur trilled from somewhere across the room. "What adventures we could have. This is like one of those country house mysteries, where everybody's locked up together. I do wonder who will play the victim. What if I found the body? I wonder if I'd faint?"

Somebody, Jane thought it was Uncle Joe, said, "Shut up."

"Could you make anything of the weather reports on the radio?" Jane asked Shelley around a mouthful of toothpaste when they got to their rooms.

"Too much static. But it's a typical spring storm. It'll clear off by morning."

The wind howled and a branch broke and slithered down the roof. Jane and Shelley blindly felt their way back to their rooms. Jane shuddered and she got into her long flannel nightgown.

"Too bad there wasn't any chance of talking to Eden about the treasure," Shelley said, calling from the next room.

"We can catch her sometime tomorrow," Jane said. She took another quick glance at her notebooks and then settled in with a mystery book she'd brought along, which was a challenge to read by the flickering kerosene lamplight. She could hear Shelley puttering around in her own room. Probably cleaning things. Shelley was an inveterate cleaner-upper.

After a bit, Jane realized the temperature had dropped and it was getting really chilly. She opened her doorway to the hall. "There's a very bad draft out here. I wonder if a door's been left ajar?"

There was a low wailing sound from somewhere.

"What was *that!*" Shelley exclaimed, rushing through the bathroom to Jane's room.

Jane was wide-eyed. "I don't know. I don't hear it now."

"Open the door again," Shelley said.

The wail began again. Jane started to laugh, albeit a bit nervously. "It's the wind down this hall. I lived in a dormitory once that was like that. Get the right combinations of doors along the hall opened and a good wind outside and you get an eerie howling noise."

"You're real certain that's what it is?"

"Certain enough that I'm not going to go check it out."

Shelley went back through the bathroom that led to her room.

A minute later, Jane called through, "I'm in charge here. I do have to check it out."

"Want me to go along?" Shelley was trying to read a magazine by the light of her small bedside kerosene lamp.

"No, of course not," Jane said, mentally pleading, *Please insist on joining me!*

But Shelley took her at her word. Jane put on a robe, lighted her lamp, and opened the door again. The howling, which wasn't audible with the door shut, sounded louder and more ominous. *Don't be a big baby,* Jane told herself. *Just check that the main doors are locked and don't go all spooky and stupid.*

This resolve lasted down the hallway and into the main room. As Jane approached the front door, which was open slightly, an enormous gust of rain-laden wind blew it all the way open. The heavy door crashed against the wall, and bounced back, nearly smacking Jane in the process. The wind had blown out her lamp, which she set down on the floor.

She closed the door, tested it, and discovered that the latch was old and didn't quite fit. After a bit of experimenting, she discovered that closing the door, then flinging herself against it, caused a nice snick as the bolt actually went home. Now that she'd solved the door problem, all she had to do was go back to her room.

In the dark.

Without a lamp.

Or flashlight.

But there was lightning. And if she got her bearings with each flash and took it slowly, she could return without running into anything. She stood quite still, peering blindly into the main room, ready to get a good fix on just where she was the next time there was a flash of light.

Something brushed against her ankle.

Jane screamed just as a great noisy blast of sound and light seemed to strike only feet away. Over the sound of her heart thudding, she could hear the distinct ripping sound of a big limb peeling off a tree outside the house.

There was a creature in the house. A raccoon? A possum? Or something bigger and scarier. Or, worse yet, a person! But what would a person be doing at ground level? Crawling? The thought gave her the creeps even worse.

She tried shuffling briskly in the direction she thought she needed to go, but cracked her foot against a chair leg. She was disoriented. There shouldn't have been a chair there. Dear God, why hadn't she brought along a flashlight?

Something bumped her leg again.

And meowed.

Jane nearly collapsed with relief. She'd seen the big gray tabby cat earlier in the afternoon, once when it was snoozing on an easy chair and again when it wandered up the steps just after dinner. She knelt down and said, "Kitty? Kitty?"

"Mrrreow," the cat said chummily.

She picked it up, with a loony sense of comfort.

"Now," she told it, "we're going to go back to my room. Very slowly, very carefully. You can probably see perfectly well in here, but I can't, so I'd appreciate it if you'd tell me if I'm about to run into something."

"Mrrreow." It sounded like consent to Jane in her fevered state.

Another flash of lightning. The cat and Jane both tensed, but it gave her a few more feet of movement. But when the lightning flash was over, there was the flicker of another light. Right in her eyes. Someone had turned on a flashlight, and seeing her, quickly turned it back off.

"Who's there?" she called down the length of the main room.

Her only answer was another rumble of thunder.

This was not good. There might be half a dozen reasons someone else was roaming around the house, but no good reason for not responding when spoken to.

She kept her blind gaze directed at the direction the light had come from and the next time the room was briefly illuminated by the storm, she cast a quick, thorough look around the far end of the room. But there was no sign of anyone. There was so much furniture that whoever it was could have just ducked behind a sofa or chair, waiting for Jane to leave.

Which was precisely what she intended to do. As quickly as possible.

Still holding the cat, which was purring as if nothing were wrong at all, Jane made her way, a few feet at a time, back to the door leading to the hallway where the tiny guest rooms were. She was feeling her way along the left-hand wall, trying to remember which door was hers, when the cat suddenly hissed.

Someone bumped into them and quickly fled. The footsteps were soft, perhaps made by socks or slippers or bare feet, but distinctly footsteps.

Jane, still holding onto the cat, plunged into the next doorway she came to, hoping desperately that it was her own bedroom.

It was.

"Where have you been all this time?" Shelley called. "Jane?" Shelley got out of bed and came through the bathroom. "Good Lord! You're as pale as a ghost. And what are you doing with that cat?"

Jane sat down on her bed and the cat settled in her lap. "I've had a real adventure," she said breathlessly.

She recounted to Shelley how the main door had all but attacked her, her lamp had blown out, the cat had scared her half to death, and someone who would not answer had shined a flashlight at her.

"Jane, are you quite certain your imagination hasn't just gone into overdrive?" Shelley asked.

"Yes, and I'm not finished yet. Out there in the hallway, when I was almost to my door, somebody ran into me. And I didn't imagine it because the cat hissed at him or her."

"Okay," Shelley said briskly. "We'll just get to the bottom of this right now. I'll get my flashlight. Keep the cat in here so we don't trip over him."

Pajama'd and robed, and equipped with Shelley's powerful flashlight, they set out. There was no one in the hallway, but there was a light shining under the door to Aunt Iva's room. Jane tapped lightly on the door. There was a scuffling sound and some whispering behind the door and finally Iva said, "Who's there?"

"It's Jane Jeffry, Miss Thatcher."

The door opened a crack. Iva's wig was badly off center. "What is it?"

"Have you been out of your room recently?"

"Of course not. Why would I be?"

"Maybe to get a snack from the kitchen?" Jane suggested. "Did you hear anyone in the hallway here?"

"I did not," Iva said, rudely shutting the door in Jane's face.

"Let's go look over the main room," Shelley said.

The room looked just as it had before the power went out earlier in the evening. At least Jane thought so. But Shelley was more observant. She directed her light along the far wall. "Something's missing."

Jane stared. "The pictures are gone. Weren't there a couple hunting prints or something on that wall?"

"Yes," Shelley said. "And I looked at them. They were trite and worthless. Who would steal them? And why?"

"I don't know, but it explains why somebody was in here and wouldn't answer me, doesn't it?"

"Maybe," Shelley said, sounding a bit shaken now herself. She shined her light around the rest of the room. They looked behind chairs and found no sign of anyone lurking. "Let's go back to bed. This is going to all seem very silly in the morning."

"I sincerely hope so. But I don't like spooky stuff and this whole night has been spooky to the max. And I can't imagine why the person who shined the flashlight on me wouldn't answer when I called out. Somebody's up to no good here."

"Jane, you just concentrate on the wedding and quit worrying about what anybody else is up to. Everything's going to work out just fine."

"No power, no bridesmaids' dresses, a flock of squabbling old ladies, a cat burglar, and everything's going to be fine?" Jane said. "Like hell."

❖

Chapter 6

Larkspur was the one to find the body.

He did not faint.

He tapped quietly, but frantically, at Jane's bedroom door at seven in the morning. "Jane, I have very bad news," he said. All his artifice had dropped away and he looked ten years older. "I was up early and thought I'd look at the stairs to see if there was a way to wind some flowers around the banister—"

"You woke me up to talk about flowers?" Jane asked.

"No, no. I was just explaining how I came to find her."

"Who 'her'?"

"Mrs. Crossthwait. She's dead."

Jane, still half asleep, just stared at him, trying to take in what he was saying. "Dead? Mrs. Crossthwait's dead?" she whispered.

"At the bottom of the staircase. She must have fallen."

"Have you called for an ambulance?" Jane asked.

"Yes. And the police. I think she should be covered up so no one else sees her that way," Larkspur said.

"I'll dress and be right there," Jane said.

She woke Shelley and they flung on clothing, grabbed the comforter off Jane's bed, and joined Larkspur in the main room.

"No, no quilt," Larkspur said. "I've been thinking. It could contaminate evidence."

"Evidence?" Jane exclaimed. "Evidence of what? What are you talking about?"

Shelley said, "Larkspur's right. What if she didn't just fall?"

"Are you two suggesting somebody actually killed her?" Jane asked.

"Not suggesting," Larkspur said. "But it's always a possibility."

Mrs. Crossthwait lay face-down on the bottom two steps, her neck twisted at an impossible angle. She wore a long cotton nightgown with red and white stripes and a somewhat yellowed white robe over it. There was a pink slipper halfway up the stairway and another on her right foot. Jane turned away, trying not to gag. "I think we should at least put up a barrier of chairs. If I were dead, I wouldn't want people gawking at me. Thank heaven there's no one else staying in the upstairs rooms yet who would have to edge around a body to come down."

The three of them moved some furniture, but Jane's hope that Mrs. Crossthwait could be quietly removed before anyone else was up and about was dashed by the sirens on the ambulances and the police car that arrived a few minutes later. Iva and Marguerite came stumbling into the main room, their wigs askew. "What's going on?" Iva asked. "Is there a fire? Should we leave the building?"

"No," Jane said, doing her best to shoo them back to

their rooms. "There's been an accident. The seamstress fell down the steps."

"Is she badly hurt?" Marguerite said. "I did a little nursing in my youth. I might be able to help—"

"There's no helping her, I'm afraid," Jane said.

"She's dead?" Iva screeched. "Someone has died here just before dear Livvy's wedding?"

Wedding, Jane thought. *Dresses. Somebody would have to finish the dresses!* Then she felt guilty. The poor old woman was dead and all Iva and Jane were thinking of was the wedding. Still, she had to ask. "Do either of you sew well?"

"I do," Iva said.

Mr. Willis, in a shocking red silk dressing gown, nearly knocked the old women down as he careened through the door. "What is it! Not a fire!"

Jane left Iva and Marguerite to explain the situation to him while she went to open the door to the ambulance. She could see Uncle Joe sprinting out from the woods. He could really move when necessary, she thought sourly.

The two men and a woman from the ambulance rushed past her and a tall, blond Viking of a police officer followed. Eden, Layla, and Kitty had joined the knot of people at the door to the bedroom hallway. Shelley and Larkspur stood with Jane at the front door. In a few minutes, the police officer joined them and introduced himself as John Smith.

"A likely story," Larkspur said with a nervous laugh.

Officer Smith ignored him. "Who's in charge here?" he asked.

"I guess I am," Jane said. "This is the early contingent of a wedding party and I'm the planner." She gave him her name and home address.

"And did you find the body?"

"No, I did," Larkspur said.

"And you are—?"

"The florist. Larkspur."

"A likely story," Officer Smith said without a trace of a smile. "And you put in the call for us?"

"Yes. I was up early. Couldn't sleep. I put some coffee on, then came in here while I waited because I wanted to consider putting flowers on the stairs. I saw her—" He shuddered.

"Did you touch the body?"

"No. Oh, no! I could tell she was dead, and even if she hadn't been, I wouldn't have known what to do."

Officer Smith turned back to Jane. "Who is the woman?"

Jane gave Mrs. Crossthwait's name and agreed to supply him with an address and phone number. To all other questions—next of kin, age, and such—Jane had no answers.

"Do any of you have any reason to suspect foul play?" the officer asked.

"No, of course not!" Jane said. "She was old and not very steady on her feet and she must have come down the stairs overnight and lost her footing. The stairs are very slippery, as you can see."

Officer Smith made a note of her comments.

Shelley cleared her throat meaningfully. "I don't mean to be an alarmist or troublemaker, but—"

"You are—?" Smith asked.

"Shelley Nowack. I live next door to Jane and came along to help with the wedding. I just wanted to mention that I watched Mrs. Crossthwait go up the stairs twice yesterday and she was extremely wary and cautious. She held onto the banister with both hands and took each step very slowly. I can't imagine her just skipping lightly down the stairs in the dark. I didn't see a flashlight anywhere near her and the power was out overnight."

Officer Smith made more notes.

Shelley said, "Jane, don't you have something to contribute?"

Jane sighed. "Okay, okay. I came out here late last night because the front door had blown open. When I started to return, I saw someone at that end of the room. Well, I didn't see them, exactly. But somebody was there and shined a flashlight in my eyes for a second, then wouldn't answer when I asked who was there."

"And what did you do then?" Smith asked.

"I picked my way through the dark to my room. Shelley and I came back here with a flashlight, but there wasn't anybody in here. We went to bed," Jane said. "I assumed somebody couldn't sleep. Was maybe coming down to the kitchen to get a glass of milk or something, and just didn't feel like talking to me."

"When was this?" Officer Smith asked.

Shelley and Jane glanced at each other. "I didn't look at my watch," Jane said, "but it must have been about ten-thirty."

"And there wasn't a body on the steps then?" the officer inquired.

"Of course not!" Jane said.

"But there might have been another reason for somebody to be roaming around in here," Shelley said, urging Jane along. "The pictures. Remember?"

"Oh, yes. When we came back out here with a flashlight, the pictures on that wall were missing—"

They all turned to look where she was pointing. The pictures were all back in place.

Without a word, Smith went back to the other end of the room and talked briefly with the ambulance attendants. They had been getting ready to put Mrs. Crossthwait on a stretcher, but now sat down on a couple of nearby chairs while Smith used a mobile phone.

"Now we've done it," Jane said. "This guy is going to think somebody bumped her off and we'll have police all over the place."

"Police at the Wedding," Shelley said. "Isn't that the title of a book?"

"Police at the Funeral. Allingham," Jane said, preoccupied. "Nobody had any reason to harm her. Except me, maybe. And I certainly wouldn't have shoved her down the stairs. At least not before she finished the dresses."

"It's out of our hands," Larkspur said. "Always better to be honest, you know. Even if it is a nuisance. I wonder if I can go now. I've got to get back to the city and get the flowers."

"I wouldn't ask for a while yet," Shelley said.

The police were very thorough. A photographer showed up and took pictures of Mrs. Crossthwait's body, the stairs, the stair rails, and the upper landing from every possible angle. A severe-looking middle-aged woman turned up with a fingerprint kit and coated the banister with dust and took prints of everybody else. Nobody regarded this with favor and Iva threw a full-blown fit, but ended up having her fingerprints taken anyway. Another police officer arrived and began questioning everyone.

The power had been restored, and Mr. Willis, doing a real loaves and fishes act, managed to prepare breakfast for everyone, guests and law officers as well.

"What are all these dreadful people doing here?" Iva complained. "You'd think it was a murder or something."

"I think they're just being overenthusiastic about assuring themselves it wasn't," Jane said as soothingly as she could manage.

"Do you think they suspect 'foul play,' as they put it, Shelley?" Jane asked later when they went outside for a breath of fresh air.

"I don't know. Maybe they're just bored out here in the country and are hoping for something juicy to get their teeth into."

"There's really no reason to think it wasn't just an accidental fall, is there?" Jane said, then thought for a moment. "Although you were right about her being extraordinarily cautious about going up the stairs. She took them with baby steps. Maybe she was sleepwalking."

"Or maybe you were right when you told Iva they were just making sure," Shelley said. "The fact is, there's nothing we can do about what the police think. But the dresses have to be finished."

"The police wouldn't let me in her room to see how far along she was with the sewing," Jane said. "They said I'd have to wait another hour at least. I'm going to call Mel. He was going to come up here tomorrow anyway. I'd feel better about all this if he were here."

"You mean you'd know more because he's a detective and they'll tell him things."

"Same thing," Jane said.

* * *

"An elderly woman took a tumble down the stairs and you want me to come up there and butt in?" Mel said a little later.

Jane was almost whispering into the phone. "I'm not sure it was an accident, Mel, and the local people are acting like it's the Crime of the Century."

"That sounds like a little bit of an exaggeration," Mel said.

"Maybe a little. But Mel, I've invested four months of my life planning this damned wedding and—"

"Okay. I'm off today anyhow. But I'm just going to introduce myself to the local people. That's all. If they want to talk to me, fine. If not, I'm not going to interfere. How do you do this, Jane? It seems everywhere you go, there are dead bodies."

"It's certainly not deliberate," she said huffily. Then, because she was asking him a favor, softened it with, "I'd just like to see you a littler earlier than planned."

Detective Mel VanDyne seemed to find this very funny.

The rest of the morning was too hectic for Jane to find time to brood, much as she would have liked to sit down with Shelley and puzzle out Mrs. Crossthwait's death. Larkspur managed to escape to fetch his flowers from the shop. Aunt Iva and Layla volunteered to whip together the last of the dressmaking jobs. Mrs. Crossthwait had made some remarkable progress during the evening before her death. There was little but hemming and putting on hooks and buttons to do and they both proclaimed themselves willing and able to do these jobs. The only holdup was trying to get into Mrs. Crossthwait's room.

Before the ambulance people were allowed to gather up the body, Mr. Willis's skivvy sneaked away from him, told the medical workers how ill she felt, and was tentatively diagnosed as possibly having an appendicitis attack. Jane thought Mr. Willis was going to have a stroke when he was told that he was losing her. Kitty and Eden reluctantly agreed to help out in the kitchen until he could find a replacement.

There was a lot of mean-spirited jockeying for possession of the one phone between him and everyone else who had calls to make. Both Iva and Marguerite seemed to have a wide circle of friends they felt honor bound to keep in touch with on a daily basis.

"It's unraveling," Jane nearly wept. "All my work, all my meticulous planning, and it's falling to bits."

"Nonsense!" Shelley said briskly. "These things happen in clumps. Nothing more will go wrong now. Bad things happen in threes, you know."

"Then why are we up to five or six?" Jane asked.

Shelley ignored the query. "You've already had all the bad luck and it'll be clear sailing from now on."

"You know you don't believe that," Jane said.

"No, not really. But I thought you'd like to hear it. Soldier on, Jane. Just soldier on."

The equipment rental people arrived as the two ambulances pulled out of the parking area—one with Mrs. Crossthwait, the other with the skivvy, who was now screaming with pain. The driver of the truck seemed seriously alarmed by this.

"It's nothing," Jane lied. "Just an appendicitis attack."

"Two of them?"

"No, just one," Jane said curtly, feeling that he might

flee if informed that the other vehicle was transporting the body of another employee.

Jane was enormously pleased that there seemed to be no hitches with this stage of preparation. There were three men on the truck. Two immediately got busy hauling in a table to go in the side room where the bridal shower and bachelor party would be held. The tables and chairs for the main room wouldn't arrive until the morning of the wedding because there was nowhere to store them. The third man brought the folding chairs that were placed in the side room where the bridal shower and bachelor party would take place today. The chairs were wooden, painted a rich shade of ivory, and had real fabric seats and backs.

"Good choice, Jane," Shelley said, watching and nodding.

Jane was too weak with relief to reply. One thing, at least, was going right.

The rental people were providing the linens, plates, and silverware for these events as well. Mr. Willis had made the selection of these items, with Jane's approval. The rental company workers would come back and set up the main room the next morning, remain during the wedding ceremony itself, and be ready to whisk the chairs away as soon as the bridal party went outdoors for pictures and set up the buffet table and then hang around somewhere until it was all over and they could take everything away. It was expensive to have them hanging around for so long, but given the available space, there had been no alternative.

"See," Shelley said smugly. "I told you everything was going to work out from here on."

Mr. Willis appeared at Jane's side, looking considerably less frazzled. "That Uncle Joe person has found me two local women who will come in and replace my help," he said. "But it's going to cost a little more."

"I don't care," Jane said. "Hire them."

"Better and better," Shelley said. "You deserve a break now that everything's back under control. There's somewhere I want you to go with me."

"Where's that?"

"Wanda's Bait and Party Shoppe. I can't miss the chance to see it."

❖

Chapter 7

They sought out Eden to show them the way. "Thank goodness! I'd like to get away from here for a while," she said. "The aunts are driving me bonkers."

"Speaking of the aunts," Jane said. "They were up to something late last night."

"What kind of something?" Eden asked, trying (and failing) to hide her surprise at the state of Jane's terrible old station wagon.

Jane caught the look. "I could afford something better," she said. "I just hate to shop. As for the aunts, I have no idea. I tapped on Iva's door to ask her something and there was a lot of rustling and whispering before she opened it a bare inch."

"A greedy scheme, no doubt," Eden said. "They're always trying to con somebody out of something. It never works. Never. But that doesn't discourage them. They're weird old things. Marguerite must have been quite a number when she was young. My dad says she was a stunning beauty once, and had whole flocks of suitors. Dad's never admitted it, but I think he might have been one of them. But Iva never married."

"Why is that?" Shelley asked from the backseat of the station wagon as they turned onto the main road.

"I don't think she found one rich enough," Eden said. "That's just a guess though. She anticipated being very wealthy in her own right someday when their father, Oliver Wendell Thatcher, popped off. And she had Marguerite as a bad example."

"Bad example of what?" Jane asked.

"Getting taken to the cleaners by a man. Marguerite fell head over heels for an Englishman my dad always said reminded him of Bertie Wooster without the money. Rowe, his name was. Percival? Lancelot? Tristram? Something classic and silly. He claimed, in a convincingly bumbling way, to be the scion of an ancient British family. Very posh stuff for a snob like Marguerite. So she married him without checking this out thoroughly enough."

"How many of us do that!" Shelley said with a laugh.

"Marguerite should have. It turned out that he was the great-great nephew or second cousin three times removed of an 'honorable,' which I think is the lowest rank of the aristocracy, and that his line of the family had been fishmongers. Or maybe it was eel fishers. Something to do with slimy water creatures. By the time Marguerite figured out why he kept dawdling about taking her to see the 'family estate' back in Merry Olde England, he'd spent nearly all her money. Marguerite went to O. W. for more and he said he'd only give her enough to get a divorce. Which she did."

"And she never remarried?" Shelley asked.

"Nope. Once was plenty. Turn right at the next corner,

Jane. And Iva has never let poor old Marguerite forget her mistake."

"You said she expected to be rich when O. W. died," Jane said. "She wasn't?"

"Oh, yes. All three of them, Iva, Marguerite, and Jack, inherited a lot. Well, a lot by most people's standards," Eden said. "Take the right-hand fork at the bottom of the hill. But they'd all expected it to be much more. Jack got the company, of course. Iva and Marguerite got some stocks and a couple of pieces of good commercial property in downtown Chicago that's given them both generous incomes. But they were expecting something along the lines of what the Sultan of Brunei might leave. They had an extremely exaggerated idea of what their old daddy was worth."

"Oh! The treasure story!" Jane exclaimed. "I wanted to ask you about it."

"Treasure? Oh, the secret treasure! I'd almost forgotten that," Eden said. "Where did you hear about it?"

"Larkspur. The florist. He mentioned having heard about a treasure at the lodge."

Eden waved this fantasy away. "There was talk of hidden riches years ago when O. W. died. Mainly put about by Iva and Marguerite to explain why they weren't fabulously wealthy, I think. Jack never bought the theory, though. He told my dad he'd expected there to be more, too, but thought O. W. had spent all the rest of the money on women. He was quite the old roué. Nearly eighty when he died, I think, and still had two mistresses."

"You're kidding!" Shelley exclaimed.

"Well, they probably weren't technically mistresses anymore," Eden said with a laugh. "One was in her fifties, the other sixty-something. But O. W. had supported them both for decades and Jack, to his credit, continued to pay for their apartments and give them an allowance."

"Does he still?" Jane asked.

Eden shrugged. "I have no idea. I never thought to ask my dad if Jack kept it up. They may not still be living. O. W. died about fifteen years ago and they weren't spring chickens. Anyway, that's probably where the rest of the fortune went. There might have been any number of other women as well who benefitted from old O. W.'s hormonal largesse."

"So there's no treasure?" Shelley asked.

"Oh, I guess there could be," Eden said. "But if there had been, surely somebody would have found it by now. And Jack must have gone through his father's records very closely. It would be tricky to convert very much cash to something secret without having a paper trail. Oh, Jane, turn left here."

Wanda's Bait and Party Shoppe was something of a disappointment. It was a tiny combination of convenience store, old-fashioned dime store, and sports shop. Everything was dusty and antiquated, including the elderly clerk who they assumed was Wanda herself. Shelley bought a fishing reel for her husband Paul in the belief that it might actually be an antique that he'd get a kick out of.

Jane found a tube of Tangee lipstick. "It's probably dried up into a little orange pebble," she admitted, "but I used to love the stuff. My mother wore it and the smell was wonderful."

When they got back in the car, Jane said, "I don't suppose there's a McDonald's anywhere near, is there? I need a hash brown. Comfort food."

Eden wrinkled her nose. "Those things are greasy, salty, and starchy."

"That's what I said. Comfort food."

They found one on the main highway and Shelley and Eden had coffee while Jane wolfed down her food. "I've been thinking about this treasure," Shelley said. "What could you convert cash into that wouldn't be obvious?"

"Jewels?" Eden suggested. "They'd be easy to conceal without taking up obvious space. Or a rare stamp collection? Stamps are small and flat and can be worth a lot."

"You could buy bonds and hide them," Jane said after some thought. Suddenly her eyes lit up. "The missing pictures!"

"What missing pictures?" Eden asked.

"Those hunting scenes in the main room of the lodge," Jane explained. "Last night they were missing. This morning they were back in place. If the aunts really do believe there's a treasure, they might have been taking the pictures apart to see if some kind of valuable documents or stamps were hidden behind them. That would explain all the rustling and whispering."

"Wait a minute," Shelley said. "We're putting the cart before the horse. Why would O. W. have hidden anything in the first place?"

Eden had the answer to that. "Tax scam."

Shelley nodded. "Oh, right. To pass valuable stuff on to his heirs without paying estate and inheritance taxes. Of course. Okay, I'll buy that. But if he had invested big sums in something secret, why didn't he tell them about it?"

Eden shrugged. "If it happened at all, maybe he just told Jack, not trusting the aunts to manage their money well without Jack supervising." She thought for a moment.

"No, probably not. After O. W. died, Jack did some pretty heavy borrowing to bring Novelties up to speed. New warehouses, computerized ordering, color catalogs instead of the old crummy newsprint black and white—that kind of thing. My dad invested in Jack and Novelties back then, and has always been pretty smug about how well it paid off. If Jack had possessed a secret fortune, he could have used it instead of borrowing."

"Maybe not," Shelley commented. "That would have been a tip-off to the I.R.S. that there was some financial hanky-panky going on."

Eden leaned back and frowned. "It's all so long ago. And because my dad didn't believe there was a treasure, I guess I didn't either. It would be fun if there were one, though. Oh . . . I think O. W. went a bit gaga at the end. A stroke or something. Hung on for another six months or so, but was a bit on the vegetable side."

"Which could account for why he didn't tell anyone about the treasure—if there really was one," Shelley said. "He could have simply forgotten about it."

"I still don't see how you could hide a lot of money from the I.R.S. that way," Jane said. "It would be bound to show up in the bookkeeping somewhere, wouldn't it?"

Shelley shook her head. "Not if you're patient and determined. Say the old boy had taken a thousand dollars a month out of his income every month for years and years. There are people who like to buy with cash and always have a lot around. Even the government can't keep a person from doing that with their own money. And once it comes out of the accounts, it's 'invisible' in a way. If the Feds ask what became of the money, the old boy could have said he used it on expensive dinners for friends, or just act vague and say he frittered it away. Or gave it anonymously to charity or handed it out to homeless people. It would be impossible to prove otherwise."

"Shelley, I didn't know you had such a sneaky streak!" Jane said.

"Of course you did," Shelley replied. "I spend a lot of my free time fantasizing about good ways to beat the I.R.S. You know what's wrong with this whole treasure theory?"

"What?" Eden and Jane asked like a chorus.

"Uncle Joe. I get the impression he's been there since the beginning of time."

Eden nodded. "As long as I can remember."

"Well, if there were something valuable in the lodge, wouldn't he have stumbled on it by now? Even if he weren't looking for it?"

"I think you're right," Eden said. "If Iva and Marguerite blabbed about it so much that even a florist from the city has heard the story, surely Uncle Joe has heard it."

"And if he'd found it, would he still be there?" Shelley asked.

Eden shook her head. "He'd be lounging on the beach somewhere in the Caribbean. At least, I would be, if it were me."

Jane nodded sadly. "It's interesting and kind of fun to imagine a treasure, but hard to make it work in practical terms. Especially since the building's being torn down this summer. If Uncle Joe thought there were something valuable there that he hadn't yet found, he'd be tearing the place apart in a panic by now."

"And the lodge part of the story could be wrong, too," Eden said. "If you were trying to keep something valuable hidden away, it would seem logical to keep it where you could check on it pretty frequently. I don't know if O. W. spent a lot of time out here in the later years of his life."

Shelley sighed as she stood up. "You're right. And we'd best go back. At least this speculation's kept me from fretting about Mrs. Crossthwait for a while."

"Me, too," Jane said. "And that makes me feel guilty."

"Why should it?" Eden asked, tossing her coffee cup in the trash and gathering up her purse and scarf. "She wasn't a relation. Not even a friend. Just a business connection who really wasn't doing her job."

"True. I guess I feel bad because it happened on my 'watch.' I shouldn't have put an elderly lady upstairs," Jane said.

"Where else could you have put her?" Shelley asked. "If she'd gotten the dresses finished on schedule, you wouldn't have had to put her anywhere. And it's too late now for fretting about it."

Jane acknowledged that both women were right. It really wasn't her fault that Mrs. Crossthwait had died.

But she couldn't help but wonder if it might have been someone else's.

❖

Chapter 8

When they got back to the lodge, Eden said, "If I can tear the phone away from Mr. Willis and the aunts, I'll give my dad a call and see if he remembers anything more about the supposed treasure. By the way, he can't be here for the wedding after all. My dad, I mean. Some joint venture he and Jack Thatcher own is having trouble and naturally Jack couldn't run off to see to it right now."

Jane and Shelley remained in the car, reluctant to throw themselves back into the wedding plans. "Do you think Mrs. Crossthwait's fall was an accident?" Jane asked.

Shelley thought for a long time. "I hope so," she finally said. "I don't think I could bear to think of anybody in the house actually being a killer."

"If it *was* murder, it wouldn't necessarily have to be someone in the house. There are already friends and relatives gathering at that motel in town. And the family all knows where the place is," Jane said. "The front door was open, remember?"

Shelley frowned. "Jane, you're right about opportunity.

But the important consideration is motive. Mrs. Crossthwait was a mildly irritating old lady. Nothing more. She apparently had no connection to the Thatcher family or friends except that someone recommended her to Livvy, right?"

"Uh-huh. But you heard her last night saying she'd made a wedding dress for Marguerite. So there is at least one connection."

"If it was true," Shelley said. "And even if it was, why would Marguerite have bumped her off for making a dress half a century ago?"

"Good point," Jane admitted.

"So if someone did topple her down the stairs, it had to be someone from her own circle of relatives, neighbors, friends. None of whom are involved in this wedding."

"That we know of," Jane said ominously.

"What on earth do you mean by that?"

"Just that we don't know much about her. What if she was one of old O. W.'s elderly mistresses?"

Shelley whipped her head around. "Oh, my gosh! You couldn't think so!"

"No, I don't, really. But anything's possible. You said it yourself, Shelley, to Officer Smith. She was terribly cautious of the stairs. She went up them like a crab, with both hands on the rail, getting both feet on each step before going on to the next one. This isn't a woman who would dream of skipping down the steps in the dark."

"Maybe not. But you're ignoring the nosiness factor. Maybe she heard whoever was down there and shined the flashlight on you, and simply couldn't resist investigating. Or possibly she'd left something really important to her—medication or such—in her car and it was vital enough to her to take the risk. She was too busy shrieking during dinner to eat much. Maybe she just got so hungry that she risked the stairs."

"Maybe," Jane said.

"Not maybe. Probably," Shelley said firmly. "And you have to quit worrying about it and get your mind back on the wedding."

Further speculation was cut off by the arrival of more of the wedding party. An enormous, shining black luxury car was first. Livvy herself was in the passenger seat and Jane assumed the distinguished-looking driver was her father, Jack Thatcher. She and Shelley hopped out of the station wagon and went to meet them.

Jack Thatcher was a handsome, silver-haired man with a golf tan, casual but expensive clothing, and an arrogant air of being a "captain of industry." Livvy insisted on introducing her father to Jane even though he clearly wasn't interested in meeting the hired help.

"Ah, Mrs. Jeffry. You've been helping Livvy plan the wedding," he said, appearing to dismiss her with the rest of the necessary riffraff.

Helping? Jane thought. *There wouldn't have been a wedding without me.*

"Yes, I've 'helped' a bit," she said. Her tone should have warned him, but it didn't.

"The van following us has the wedding gifts," he said. "You can set them out for display."

"I beg your pardon?" Jane said. "This is the first I've heard of this. I hadn't planned—"

"You'll find a place for them," he said.

Jane could think of a perfect place, but it would be vulgar to suggest it.

"Mr. Thatcher, I'm sorry to say that just isn't done anymore," Jane said, then recklessly added, "I believe in most circles, it's considered ostentatious and in poor taste."

He'd leaned into the car to pick up some paperwork and now turned and glared at her. "You dare tell me—"

"Daddy!" Livvy all but screamed. "It's *my* fault. I forgot to tell Jane you wanted the gifts displayed. We'll find somewhere to put them. Maybe on tables in the upstairs hallway."

"Do whatever you like, Livvy. It's your wedding," he said, clearly not meaning a word of it.

Now that Jane and Jack Thatcher had pretty well established themselves as enemies, she decided to let him have the bad news as bluntly as possible.

"Mr. Thatcher, there was a death here last night."

"What?"

"The seamstress fell down the stairs and died. I'm afraid the police may want to discuss it with you."

"With me? Why? I don't even know this person."

"It did happen on your property," Jane said.

"Mrs. Crossthwait is dead?" Livvy asked. "That's awful. What happened? What can we do?"

"It's not up to us to do anything," Jack said. "There was no reason for her to be here that I can imagine. If Mrs. Jeffry invited her, Mrs. Jeffry can sort it out."

He strode off, flapping his paperwork angrily against his leg. Livvy gave Jane a frantic, upset look, then went running after her father calling, "Daddy . . . wait . . ."

Shelley took hold of Jane's arm. "Sit down right here and now. You're as white as a sheet. We can't have you fainting from fury."

"What makes him think he can talk to me like that—"

The rest of the sentence stuck in her throat as she swallowed back a sob of frustration.

"He's just a hateful bastard, Jane."

"I'm tempted to just pack my bag and go home," Jane said, her voice shaking. "Let *him* put on the damned wedding."

"You know you won't do that," Shelley said. "You're not a quitter."

"Neither am I a medieval serf! That . . . that . . ."

"Jerk?"

Jane shook her head. "Oh, 'jerk' doesn't even come close, Shelley. In fact, the only phrases that pop to mind are things I've heard but never said out loud. One of them starts with 'mother'—"

Before she could consider revising this lifelong record, the gift van arrived. A harassed-looking young man climbed out and asked, "Where am I supposed to put this stuff?"

"Ask Mr. Thatcher," Jane snapped.

Shelley stepped in and said in her kindliest manner, "Do you work for Mr. Thatcher?"

"I'm afraid I do," the young man said.

"See, Jane," Shelley said. "Here's someone who has to deal with him more than you do and he's not rolling around chewing sticks and frothing at the mouth."

"I've come close though," he said with a sudden grin.

Jane took a deep breath and returned the smile. "Okay, we'll find somewhere to show this stuff off. I hope all the cards are with the proper gifts. I have to give Livvy the list so she can write the thank you notes."

Jane stomped off, walking hard on her heels. Fortunately, the people who'd brought the folding chairs had an extra table along, which Jane asked them to put in the side room where the bride's shower was to be held shortly. They draped it with one of the linen sheets that had returned from the laundry the day before and Jane and Shelley hastily arranged the gifts so that the places that had been darned didn't show.

While they were setting out and drooling over the Steuben and Waterford items, Larkspur returned from the city. "What are you doing? What's this extra table? Am I supposed to floralize it? Is this that scene from *High Society?* Is someone going to burst into 'True Love' with full orchestration?"

Jane only picked up on one word and it tickled her. "Floralize? Please tell me you didn't really say that!"

Larkspur blushed slightly. "A technical term," he said. "This is so tacky, Jane. Do all these things still have their price stickers on them?"

"It's not my fault," Jane said. "Livvy's dad's idea. And if you're smart, you'll stay as far from him as you can. He'd mop the floor with you. He's already scraped the windows with me."

"Daddy Dearest?" Larkspur asked. "I love strong-minded men."

"Well, you're not going to love this one," Jane said. "And if you do, I don't want to hear about it. Ever!"

"Have you met the groom's family yet?" Larkspur asked. "They were just coming in as I drove up. Not quite crème de la crème."

"I hope this meeting goes better than the last one," Jane said. She fluffed up her hair, took a deep breath, and forced a pleasant smile as she went back to the main room. The Thatchers and the Hesslings were chatting. Jane hung back, pretending to be studying one of her notebooks rather than interrupt.

Dwayne Hessling, the groom, was easy to spot. He was a stunning young man. Curly dark hair, blue eyes, a Cary Grant cleft in his chin. But as Eden had said, there was a touch of the cheap gigolo about him. His stance was cocky, his hair a bit too long and shiny, his trousers just a bit too tight. While the others spoke, his gaze was darting around the room in an acquisitive manner.

Dwayne's brother Errol was standing next to him. He was to be the best man. Superficially, they were alike in coloring and features, but Errol was burly, and he smiled a lot and when he did, his eyes crinkled. Jane thought that Livvy had picked the wrong brother. Errol looked a lot more open and friendly and was staring at Livvy with the unabashed admiration of a hunting enthusiast for a really good dog.

The third member of the family group was their mother, Irma, who was clearly out of her element. She was a short, dumpy woman who was wearing what was probably the best dress from a cheap store. Her ensemble was a shell blouse, a skirt, and lightweight coat that might have been fashionable ten years ago if it had been linen and an attractive color. But it shouted polyester in mustard tones. She kept oozing back away from the group, and Errol kept taking her arm and bringing her back. She answered the few remarks addressed to her with a nervous giggle.

Jane felt enormously sorry for her and now understood why Irma had insisted that she and Errol would stay in the nearby motel rather than at the lodge. She'd known, or feared, she'd be out of place with the Thatcher crowd.

Dwayne was the one marrying into the Thatcher clan, not his mother.

Jack made a gesture that seemed to be an order to take a tour of the house. Livvy and the Hessling brothers followed obediently. Irma slipped the noose and sat down in a high-backed chair, took her right shoe off, and started rubbing her foot. Jane approached her and Irma hastily shoved her shoe back on with a grimace.

"New shoes," she explained. "I should have known better."

"Mrs. Hessling, I'm Jane Jeffry. I'm the wedding planner. We've corresponded."

"Yes, yes. I've appreciated you keeping me up on the plans. I'm a waitress, you know," she added as if it were relevant.

"No, I didn't know," Jane said, confused. "Uh—you must meet a lot of interesting people."

"You do," Irma Hessling said, nodding sagely. "And you learn a lot about how they think and act. That Mr. Thatcher . . . he's the kind who'd send his hamburger back if it wasn't cooked just right and then refuse to pay because of the delay."

Irma was sharper than she looked. Common sense in the place of fashion sense.

"I believe you're right," Jane said, thinking uneasily about the final payment that was due on her work at the completion. He'd probably dock her for Mrs. Crossthwait's death.

"And poor little Livvy would bury a burnt bit in her mashed potatoes before she'd complain."

Jane thought for a moment and said, "You're not very pleased about this match, are you?"

Irma leaned forward and spoke in almost a whisper. "No, not really. It's not good for anybody. 'Course, the Thatchers are rich and Dwayne likes that, but it isn't the money that's wrong. Now, Errol, he could marry a rich girl and he'd stay the same person. And he could marry a shy little thing like Livvy and treat her real nice. But Dwayne's always been bossy unless I stood on him real hard." She'd taken her shoe back off and was massaging a bunion. "And Livvy, poor thing, is used to being bossed. It's going to bring out the worst in him."

Jane took the woman's hand. "You may be right. But they're going to have to work it out themselves. Maybe when Livvy's married and has some children, she'll get a bit more backbone. Motherhood does that for a lot of women."

"I hope that's so. I really shouldn't have said anything."

"Let me know if there's anything you need or want," Jane said. The tour group was coming back and it wouldn't help either of them to be discovered in a secret little confab.

"Shelley," Jane said a little later, "I think this wedding is cursed."

Shelley, who had been helping Larkspur arrange the flowers and enjoying his outrageous flattery, was cool. "You just have pseudo-mother-of-the-bride jitters."

"I hope that's all they are," Jane said. "I need a nap and I don't see one anytime soon on my horizon."

Chapter 9

Aside from the aunts demanding better bath towels, one of the caterer's local helpers twisting her ankle, and Larkspur dropping and breaking his best flower vase, the rest of what remained of the morning went fairly well. Eden, Kitty, and Layla, under Aunt Iva's supervision, had almost finished their dresses. Probably not to Mrs. Crossthwait's exacting standards, but well enough to precede Livvy without looking bedraggled and half dressed. Mr. Willis set out a "do-it-yourself" luncheon of sandwich makings, green and pasta salads, chips, dips, and an assortment of drinks ranging from white wine to sodas to coffee. The growing crowd at the lodge helped themselves.

Jack Thatcher had assigned himself and his downtrodden assistant the job of hauling the nonresident guests back and forth from the hunting lodge to their motel. Jane tried at first to sort out who everyone was, having hand-addressed all the invitations, but soon gave up. They fell into identifiable categories though. Some of the older, better-dressed men appeared to be business associates of Jack's. A few younger women were either their middle-aged crisis replacement wives—or friends of Livvy's who were gathering for the bridal shower in the afternoon. Most of these stylish young women were probably serving in both roles, Jane thought, since Livvy seemed to be a bit short on close personal friends.

There was also a handful of young men who greeted Dwayne with slaps on the back and mildly raunchy jokes. They were friends of his who would be attending the bachelor party later in the evening.

Shelley and Jane stood by the door, introducing themselves to the newcomers as they arrived and helping them find their friends. During a lull, Shelley said, "Remember the high school rule? The prettiest girl surrounded herself by ugly friends so she could really shine in comparison."

"Hmmm. You mean that wasn't coincidence?" Jane asked with a grin.

"Seems that Dwayne has done the same," Shelley said.

Jane glanced at the small knot of young men surrounding Dwayne where he stood in a Lord of the Manor pose in front of one of the fireplaces. Jane had seen Jack Thatcher strike the same pose only hours earlier. Shelley was right: none of Dwayne Hessling's friends matched him for sheer good looks, although most of them were a little too well-dressed. Trying, she guessed, to fit in among the upper crust to the best of their budgets. Dwayne's good luck in combining romance and finance might rub off on them, they might have thought.

Jane leaned against the doorjamb and said, "I wouldn't go back and be that young now for anything. All that struggle to get ahead in life, to figure out what and who you want to be."

"And it's harder now," Shelley agreed. "Even a college degree is a requirement instead of an extra leg up in the business world. I'll bet half those boys are spending their evenings slaving away at night classes in business management or computer technology at the junior college."

"Except for Dwayne," Jane said. "Dwayne is marrying into management." She glanced around to make sure they couldn't be overheard. "And his mother isn't very happy about it."

"I'd think she'd be thrilled," Shelley said. "I sure wouldn't mind if my kids married well."

"She's too sensible to be blind to his faults, it seems." Jane repeated what she could remember of her conversation with Mrs. Hessling. "I really think she likes Livvy better than her son. No, not 'likes' exactly. But feels more protective. Even she seems to have caught on that Livvy's marrying to please her father, not herself. And that Dwayne is going to be every bit as domineering as her father."

Shelley frowned. "It's hard for us to grasp, being of somewhat pit bull mentality ourselves, but maybe that's exactly what will make Livvy happy, Jane. There are people, men and women both, who are perfectly content to abdicate responsibility. There have to be followers or nobody can be a leader."

"Waxing a tad philosophic, are we?" Jane said. "Are you suggesting Livvy's really madly in love with Dwayne?"

Shelley shrugged. "Maybe as madly as it's possible for her to be."

"Why is it I can hardly say her name without putting the word 'poor' in front of it?" Jane mused.

"Because you're a tough old broad?" Shelley suggested.

"Look who's talking!" Jane said. "You're the one who makes school principals shake with fear and car salesmen go paralytic when you walk onto the car lot."

Shelley preened a bit. "But you're getting there, Jane. You did a pretty good job of standing up to Jack Thatcher's rudeness."

Jane spotted Eden at the top of the stairs, smiling and signaling for Jane to join her. "We've got them done," Eden said when Jane and Shelley got there. "Want to see?"

The bridesmaids staged an impromptu fashion show and Jane was impressed. This wedding might not turn out to be such a catastrophe after all. Layla and Eden were young and glamorous. Kitty was young and—Jane searched for the right word and could only come up with "healthy." Their cherry-colored silk dresses literally brightened up the drab room Mrs. Crossthwait had been assigned.

"You're gorgeous! All of you. I'm so sorry you had to pitch in this way," Jane said.

"Not your fault," Eden said. "Unless you pushed Mrs. C. down the steps."

"Pushed her down the steps!" Kitty exclaimed. "Why do you say that? She just fell, didn't she?"

"I was kidding," Eden said. "Don't look so upset. It was in poor taste. Sorry."

Kitty did look offended, and didn't acknowledge the apology, but turned to Jane. "I understand the gifts have been put out on display somewhere. I brought mine along."

Jane remembered Kitty's arrival and wasn't surprised she'd brought her wedding gift along. From the looks of her luggage collection, she'd brought nearly everything she owned. Besides the two large suitcases Jane had helped her carry in when she arrived, she'd later seen Kitty bring in three cartons as well. "They're in the room where the bridal shower's going to be," Jane said. "Get back into your regular clothes and I'll show you."

A few minutes later, Jane pushed open the door of the room in question and she and Kitty were treated to the sight of Livvy and Dwayne embracing. Dwayne was kissing Livvy, who didn't appear to be participating with much enthusiasm.

"Oh, I'm sorry," Jane said. "I didn't know anyone was here."

Livvy blushed scarlet, but Dwayne just grinned and said, "Come on in. We can behave ourselves for a while. At least until tomorrow."

"Oh, Dwayne," Livvy simpered.

"Kitty brought her gift to set out," Jane explained.

"Oh, Kitty! How really lovely," Livvy said, pulling away from Dwayne and examining the cut crystal fruit bowl Kitty was holding. Livvy took it from Kitty and held it up against the light from the window. "It's just beautiful, Kitty. How good of you."

Kitty's face was utterly blank. Apparently she wasn't any better at reacting to compliments than she was at coping with bad jokes. Jane would have to remind Kitty to smile during her bridesmaid duties. Jane took the bowl from Livvy, rearranged a few other items to make room for it where the sunlight could catch in the facets, and went back to door duty with Shelley.

"The dresses are done," she said. "The girls look lovely. Even Kitty. If she'd just smile occasionally."

"Mel's here," Shelley said. "Turned up just as you went upstairs. He's in the kitchen."

"Let's assume we've done enough greeting and grab a bite of lunch before it's all gone," Jane said.

Mel was at the kitchen table, watching Mr. Willis and one of his local helpers put the luncheon leftovers away. He greeted Jane and Shelley with a rather more solemn manner than they'd expected.

"Is something wrong?" Jane asked quietly.

He shook his head. "Not a thing," he said, turning and making a subtle shushing motion.

This is not good, Jane thought.

"Jane, let's get some food and eat outside," Shelley suggested brightly. "Mel, have you eaten? Why don't you join us?"

Mr. Willis was so eager to get them out from underfoot that he quickly prepared plates for the three of them and shooed them out the door. There was a disreputable picnic table under some trees just behind the lodge and they settled there.

"So what's wrong?" Jane said before anybody could get a bite of food.

"I stopped in town to introduce myself on the way here," Mel said, looking longingly at a deviled ham sandwich. "The local police are a bit on the gabby side. Took my word for who I was and told me some interesting things." He lunged at his sandwich, determined to get at least one good mouthful before Jane started the inevitable inquisition.

"Like what?" Shelley and Jane asked as one voice.

He chewed luxuriously for a moment, took a sip of his soft drink, and sighed. "The most important is that it appears Mrs. Crossthwait was pushed pretty hard. There are faint fresh bruises that look like fingertips on her back."

"What?" Jane exclaimed. "You'd have to really put a huge amount of force behind a shove to make finger marks."

"Not if the person was on a blood thinner, apparently," Mel said. "The officer on the scene found a bottle of medicine in her purse, called the prescribing physician, and was told she had recurring incidents of phlebitis and was taking a pretty hefty daily dose of anticoagulant. That's why she bruised so easily. Now, you two chew that over while I eat."

Jane looked at Shelley. "Maybe somebody shoved her earlier."

"But why?" Shelley asked.

"Maybe by accident," Jane improvised. "If somebody else tripped, they might have put their hands out to stop their fall and ran into her instead."

Shelley rolled her eyes. "Yeah, right. And she didn't say a word of complaint? Jane, this was a woman born to complain."

"Well, I'm going to believe it until someone proves otherwise," Jane said. "I don't want to think someone deliberately pushed her down those steps to her death."

"Jane, don't be a Pollyanna," Shelley said. "It sounds to me like someone did exactly that. And I'd like the authorities to scoop him or her up before we have to spend another night in this place with the perp. I don't think there are even locks on the bedroom doors."

Jane put her elbows on the table and her head in her hands. "Okay, okay. But it wouldn't necessarily be someone who's staying here."

"The Wandering Maniac Theory?"

"No, but there are a lot of people involved in this wedding who were nearby last night. Some of the guests at the motel arrived last night. The Hesslings, for instance."

"But what could the Hesslings have had against Mrs. Crossthwait?" Shelley asked.

"What could *anybody* have had against her?" Jane countered. "Except that she was a rude old bat."

Mel was chewing thoughtfully and looking back and forth at them as if they were a tennis match.

"Nothing," Shelley said. "Nothing that I can guess, anyway. Jane, you're the only one who was seriously mad at her—don't bridle up like that—and you're also the one who had the most to gain from her staying alive and well and sewing her fingers to the bone."

"Well, *if* somebody deliberately killed her—and I don't admit I believe that—then it was someone in her own life who simply followed her out here so as to cast suspicion on somebody at the lodge. I will not allow this to have some connection to my wedding planning."

"Ah," Mel said around a potato chip. "Now I get it, Jane. You think this is going to reflect on you somehow?"

"Are the police checking on her private life?" Jane asked, not answering his question because the honest reply would sound mean-spirited, even to her.

"So far, they haven't found evidence that she had much of a life," Mel answered. "A rented apartment above a bookstore, a bit of savings but not an impressive amount. She was a childless longtime widow with Social Security, a little pension from her late husband, and her sewing money. She lived a very quiet life, the bookstore owner says. Her only visitors, as far as he knows, were the ladies she sewed for, and a couple women from her church who held an occasional meeting at her place. Oh, and she took a trip once a year in January to visit a cousin in Florida or Texas, he couldn't remember which. Somewhere warm, he said."

"But—" Jane said.

"It's too early to know more, Jane," Mel said, holding up his hand like a traffic cop trying to stop a runaway eighteen-wheeler and believing he could do it. "They only started this morning. You may be right and she has some dark secret that will come to light. But right now, the only suspects are the people who are here for the wedding."

"Swell," Jane said. "I suppose in view of these bruises, presumably from a strong malicious shove, the local police are going to be back here. Casting a pall. Questioning the guests. Making nuisances of themselves."

"Afraid so," Mel said.

"Okay," Jane said with a martyred sigh. "We can cope. I can get a grip. Figuring out a murder is, in the grand scale of things, more important than a picture-perfect wedding."

Mel muttered something that sounded like, "And a lot more interesting."

"What was that?" Jane asked.

Mel smiled. "Me? I didn't say anything."

Shelley glanced at her watch. "Almost time for the bridal shower, Jane. Eat your lunch and then we'll go make sure it goes well."

"I'll consider it to have gone well enough if everybody comes out of it alive," Jane said.

❖

Chapter 10

The bridal shower had a brittle atmosphere of forced festivity. The air crackled with high-pitched laughter. Few of the women attending really knew each other terribly well. Some of Jack's friends' trophy wives *were* acquainted and regretted it and snubbed one another in the nicest possible way. Only Layla and Eden seemed to have formed a friendly bond with Kitty on the fringes of it. The aunts were pretending that the whole plan had rested in their capable hands, and were playing the role of cohostesses with relish—which irritated the stuffing out of Jane.

She and Shelley had rounded up the guests and seen to it that the food and drinks were ready, then got out of the way. "I don't suppose we can hang around and eat?" Shelley asked. "Sort of lurk in the background and munch quietly?" The menu for the party included puff pastries with raspberry filling, rich little handmade chocolate wafers in the shape of bells, and champagne cocktails.

"There will be leftovers," Jane assured her. "And if we eat them in private, we can be much greedier. We can rub them straight onto our thighs if we want and skip the digestive process entirely. What a dismal party."

"Dismal-ish," Shelley admitted. "But that's not your fault. It's because the only thing they all have in common is poor Livvy. If you'd put on the exact same shower for Eden, for instance, it would have been fun because she has a personality. What were the little foil packages Livvy was carrying around?"

"Compacts. Really lovely things and the only decision Livvy seemed to have a strong opinion about," Jane said. "They're bridesmaid gifts. Real gold with Livvy and Dwayne's names and the date of the wedding beautifully engraved on the back. They must have cost her the earth."

"What a lovely memento," Shelley said. "At least she has good taste. Oh, that's bad of me. She's such a nice, Milquetoast sort of girl. I just want to give her a transfusion of spunk."

Jane nodded. "I'd like to like her, too. I think everyone would. What's not to like? But she's a mannequin with a complex computer system that instructs her to talk and move and act with propriety, but no sparkle."

"What's all that noise outside?" Shelley asked.

"The groom and his friends, I assume," Jane said as she and Shelley hauled themselves out of their comfortable chairs and went to check. The young men were playing touch football. Except for their size, they were indistinguishable from a bunch of fifteen-year-olds, although their language was a bit cleaner. Not much, though.

Somebody, perhaps the lethargic Uncle Joe, had dragged out a couple of lawn chairs and set them by the main door. Whether this was their destination for some reason, or they were just in transit, Jane couldn't guess.

But Jane pulled one of them in front of the door. "Sit down, Shelley. If any of the bride's party needs me, they'll be able to spot us here."

"Sure you wouldn't really rather sit a little farther away? Like somewhere in Seattle?" Shelley asked.

As they got situated, Mel and Officer John Smith emerged from the woods. They had old Uncle Joe walking between them. It was impossible to hear the conversation they were attempting to have with him, but not hard to guess the gist. Mel or the local police officer would speak. Uncle Joe would instantly shrug incomprehension. Joe's part consisted entirely of hands outspread in ignorance, negative shakes of the head, glares, and halfhearted attempts to shake the other two men off.

"He knows something about this," Jane said.

"What makes you think that?" Shelley asked, staring at the small group.

"Because he's pretending to know nothing. Nobody knows nothing."

"You can say that because you don't know my cousin Alfred."

Jane laughed. "Shelley, if somebody asks you something and you haven't got the answer, don't you at least pause and consider whether you might have some bit of information, no matter how trivial?"

"Yes, I guess so. But I'm not a cranky old recluse who isn't enjoying having his turf invaded."

"That's the point," Jane said. "It *is* his turf. In his view, anyway. He's apparently lived here, quite alone most of the time, for years. And for all his crabbing around, acting too feeble to be of any use, I think he knows every stick of furniture in the dark."

"You think he was one of the people roaming around last night during the storm?"

"I'd bet anything on it," Jane said. "And I'll bet he saw or heard things he's keeping to himself. That's why he's so vehemently denying any knowledge of what's going on here to Mel and Officer Smith. He doesn't seem to even like having family around. Imagine how he feels about The Law invading."

The cat Jane had met up with the night before came strolling around the corner and sat down to evaluate them for a long moment before taking a really serious stretch and then jumping on Jane's lap. She scritched him behind his ears.

Shelley was staring toward, but not at, the football game. She was thinking so hard, Jane could almost hear the gears grinding. Finally Shelley said, with uncharacteristic timidity, "Jane, I know this is nuts, but everybody seems to know something about this story of a hidden treasure. But nobody admits to believing in it. Don't you find that a bit suspicious?"

Jane kept petting the cat. "I guess so, but let's define 'everybody.' Layla vaguely remembered the story. Eden more so, and it was she who said the aunts came up with the theory and Jack checked it out and denies that there is one. But that's all."

Shelley shook her head. "Larkspur is roaming around with spade and shovel and a wild, greedy, non-floral gleam in his eye."

"That's right. I'd forgotten about him. How would he know?"

"We must ask," Shelley said. "If he's heard it, there are probably hundreds of other people who also have."

"So where's this leading us?"

"Well—" Shelley hesitated. "Not that I think this is necessarily right, but suppose there really is a treasure here—"

"If there were a hidden treasure," Jane interrupted, "why would it necessarily be at the hunting lodge? If I had a treasure, I'd buy a big old safe and stick it in there."

"But then it wouldn't be hidden, just locked up," Shelley said irritably. "Just hear me out, will you? Suppose there was a treasure, and it was in Mrs. Crossthwait's room. If I'd been O. W. and wanted to hide something here, I'd have hidden it in my own room or the one next to it so I could check on it while I was here, and be sure nobody else would be staying in the room when I wasn't here."

"Okay," Jane said. "I'll buy that. So you think Mrs. Crossthwait found it?"

"She seemed to be a bit on the deaf side, but her eyesight must have been a wonder. You've seen her work. All that meticulous, tiny handwork."

"But Shelley, she was here for less than a full day. How could she have found something Uncle Joe has never noticed? And if the whole Thatcher family and circle of friends plus a few strangers have heard this rumor, how could he not know about it? He's had years and years to look for it. My God! I'm starting to sound like I think it exists."

Shelley was prepared to counter this argument. "Look at the way he dresses. No one on earth has taste that bad unless they're at least color-blind."

"Wrong. My grandfather was very fond of checks, plaids, and stripes together in his old age. And he had good vision. Just no taste."

"Okay, I'll give you that one," Shelley said. "Paul's father wears the most awful hats in the world and doesn't seem to have any idea how silly he looks. But you do have to admit that Mrs. Crossthwait must have had exceptionally good vision."

"That one I agree with."

"So suppose she dropped a pin on the floor, bent over to get it, and realized the joints in the flooring formed a little door?"

"The room has a linoleum floor."

"Don't be so picky. It was just an example," Shelley snapped. "Just suppose she spotted something that didn't look quite right, investigated, and found something valuable? It could have been something very small. The corner of an envelope barely visible at the edge of a rug or something."

"What if she had?" Jane said. "We don't know enough about her to guess whether she'd just pocket it among all that stuff she brought along and live the rest of her life in luxury or whether she'd have turned it over to the rightful owner."

"The rightful owner, who is presumably Jack Thatcher, wasn't here yet when she died—"

"That we know of," Jane reminded her. "We have no idea where he was last night and it's only about an hour and a half from Chicago to here."

"—but she might have dropped a hint to someone about having found something important. She was up in that room most of the time she was here and everybody else was roaming around wherever they wanted. Anyone could have visited her up there and no one else might have even noticed."

There was a loud yelp from one of the football game participants. Jane watched in horror as two of the young men rushed over to where Dwayne Hessling was spread-eagled in the grass. But before she could act, he'd gotten up and was bending his arm experimentally. "It's okay," he said. "I can still move everything."

Jane let out the breath she'd been holding. "All we need him to do is break an arm or leg," she said.

"We'd just have to have Larkspur do something with tulips and baby's breath on his crutches," Shelley said with a laugh.

Jane gave her friend the look she usually reserved for the mother of children who were misbehaving in the grocery store. "Get back to your theory. We're already about six 'supposes' away from any sort of reality. Might as well run the whole course."

"Hmmm. To tell the truth, I'm not sure where I was going with it. Except to say that it's possible Mrs. Crossthwait saw or found something valuable and put herself in danger by mentioning it."

"You're ruining my theory that somebody who has nothing to do with this wedding discovered that she was a Nazi collaborator and followed her here to bump her off as an act of revenge," Jane said.

Shelley smiled. "Sorry about that. But why would anybody follow her here to kill her? They wouldn't know the layout of the place, especially in the dark."

"Maybe it wasn't dark all night. We had lights on in the main room when the power failed. Maybe it came back on during the night."

"But unless they'd been lurking under the furniture all

day, how would an outsider even know what room she was in?" Shelley asked.

Jane thought about this for a long moment and couldn't dredge up an argument. "Okay, okay. So if the police are right that somebody pushed her down the steps, and if it's somebody who was staying overnight, who do you suggest as chief suspect?"

"The aunts?" Shelley answered halfheartedly.

"Come on, Shelley! What threat could Mrs. Crossthwait have possibly been to either of them?"

"Well, there's the treasure story. From what we've heard, they're the ones who thought it up and the only ones, besides Larkspur, who seem to believe it. What if she found something valuable and mentioned it to them? Maybe something she didn't even recognize as being of value."

"And they wanted it for themselves, not to share with Jack, who had never believed the story to begin with . . . ?" Jane said.

"Or maybe it was just one of them," Shelley said. "One who wanted to keep it all to herself."

Jane thought about it for a while. "Maybe. But the aunts clearly snubbed her after dinner. A mere hireling daring to be chummy with them. They're really dreadful snobs."

"But last night they were the senior members of the Thatcher family present at the lodge. If she had discovered something and was being honest about it, wouldn't they be the ones she'd tell?"

"I guess so," Jane said. Then she thought for a long moment. "What if she actually knew them? Before now, I mean. Or knew of them?"

"What do you mean?"

"They're all of an age. And nobody waits until they're seventy to become a dressmaker," Jane said. "She said she'd sewn a wedding dress for Marguerite way in the past. What if her association with them caused her to know some secret about one or the other?"

Shelley's eyes lit up. "I like it," she said. "Maybe she made maternity clothes fifty years ago for the virginal-and-damned-proud-of-it Aunt Iva. They wouldn't remember someone as lowly as a seamstress, but she'd remember doing a secret job for a high society type."

"And the aunts knew perfectly well who she was and what she knew and despite their bickering, they'd stick together against an enemy."

The cat jumped off Jane's lap and walked away, as if disapproving of the conversation. Jane laughed. "So we know what the cat thinks of that theory."

"Pretty bad, huh? A bit of a stretch?" Shelley asked.

"Just a bit. Shows a good imagination though. You get an A for effort."

"Okay, forget the aunts for the moment. It's easy to imagine them destroying someone with a few well-chosen words, but not with raw physical effort. If it has to be someone here, what about Uncle Joe?"

"Motive? And let's try to stay away from secret pregnancies and Nazi connections."

"The treasure, of course," Shelley said confidently. "He's been here for ages, diligently searching, pulling up floorboards, checking the backs of drawers, peeling up bits of linoleum, pawing around in the stuffing in the animal heads, tapping on walls for secret passages—"

"Digging up the gardens?" Jane put in.

"Yes, and he's found nothing. Then this cranky old lady

whose heavy sewing machine he has to take upstairs finds the treasure. And it's going to be turned over to Jack and the aunts. Not a penny for loyal Uncle Joe. So he pushes her down the stairs, nips into her room—or wherever she said it was—and snags it."

Jane nodded. "And why would she have chosen to tell him, of all people, about it?"

Shelley slumped in her lawn chair. "Good question. Unless it was a complaint. 'Here, my good man,' " Shelley said, pretending to be Mrs. Crossthwait, " 'when you've got that sewing machine in place, get rid of that rolled-up document stuck down the throat of that awful bear rug's head.' How's that?"

Jane grinned. "Let me guess. The rolled-up document is proof that Uncle Joe was once a mass murderer."

"Or Nazi sympathizer," Shelley said cheerfully. "Take your pick."

❖

Chapter 11

One of the football players broke away from the game and went inside, nodding politely to Jane and Shelley and coming back out a few minutes later with his hands full of sodas, which he passed around. Another went inside the lodge as the first was coming out and he, too, returned a few minutes later.

"I guess I should check on how the shower is going," Jane said lethargically.

"They'd find you if they needed anything."

"Still, I need to appear to be earning my keep. Be right back. If Jack Thatcher catches me sitting down, he'll probably take a hundred bucks off my fee."

"Where is he, anyway?"

"He and his pals are off looking at a lake somewhere on the grounds, I think," Jane said. "Probably planning where the ninth green ought to be. Wait here."

"You plan to leave me here watching an amateur football game? No way," Shelley said.

As they approached the side room, Jane was pleased

to hear lots of chatter that sounded downright friendly. Apparently the earlier ice had been broken. Eden and Layla were coming out the door. Eden was heading toward the hallway to the monks' rooms, presumably for a potty break, and Layla was halfway to the kitchen. "Do you need something?" Jane asked Layla.

As she was speaking, Mr. Willis shoved open the kitchen door, balancing a tray of more champagne cocktails. "That's what I was looking for," Layla said. "We're all getting giggly-tipsy. Aunt Marguerite is telling what she considers risqué stories."

Layla looked so girlish and happy Jane had the urge to hug her. "You're having fun, aren't you?"

"If it weren't for Mrs. Crossthwait, this would have been my best weekend in years."

"You're not missing your children?"

Layla laughed. "No, not a bit. Should I feel guilty?"

"Absolutely not," Jane said.

Jane and Shelley oozed in the door and caught Livvy's eye. "Anything you need?" Jane mouthed.

Livvy was surrounded by a pile of wrapping paper and ribbons. Somebody had fetched a rather wicked-looking knife from the kitchen to help open gifts. Jane guessed nobody wanted to go to Mrs. Crossthwait's room for scissors.

Livvy pushed the paper and ribbon aside, got up, and came over. "I need a box to put everything in so none of the little things get lost. There might be some in the attic. Would you mind—?"

"Not at all," Jane said.

As she and Shelley went up the stairs, Shelley said, "She was actually smiling slightly. And it looked like a real smile."

"I can't wait for this to be over," Jane said. "Things seem to be going well now and maybe we'll just coast on through the rest."

Jane reached out to push the attic door. It wouldn't open. She tried again, thinking it was just stuck, maybe from all the rain and humidity. "That's strange. It seems to be locked."

"Locked? It wasn't locked yesterday. We looked in here, remember?"

Jane stared at the door. "How very odd. I'll see if there's a seam ripper in Mrs. Crossthwait's room."

"Is there a connection between those thoughts?" Shelley asked, trailing along.

Mrs. Crossthwait's room was a bit of a mess. The police had gone through her luggage and all her sewing materials. They hadn't deliberately vandalized the room, but it was pretty untidy. "We'll have to come back here later and pack everything up," Jane said. "Ah, here's the seam ripper. I can open the lock with it."

"What a peculiar skill," Shelley said.

"Doesn't every mother know how to get a little kid out of a bathroom when he's locked himself in?" Jane asked.

"After I had to crawl in the ground floor bathroom once to rescue Denise, I had the locks taken off," Shelley said, "and put little hooks up high so I could lock myself in, but they couldn't."

Jane took the seam ripper, went back into the hall, and sat down in front of the door, studying the lock.

"Where did you ever learn a skill like this?"

Jane smiled. "From a Frenchman that I was desperately, madly in love with."

"And you didn't marry him?"

"Couldn't. He was thirty and I was ten. My dad was attached to the embassy in Paris and we had a house outside the city. My folks wanted my sister and me to attend the local school to improve our French. A lost cause in both our cases. Monsieur Baptiste LeClerc was the math teacher. He taught us to pick locks. It was supposed to illustrate some mathematical principle, in theory. Actually, I think he was teaching us to be his accomplices. Halfway through the term, he disappeared. My mother later told me he'd been arrested for breaking into houses."

Shelley laughed. "Training you girls to be little Oliver Twists, huh?"

"He was divine. A dark sweep of hair he was always tossing back artistically. The longest, most beautiful eyelashes I've ever seen. If I'd met him as an adult, I'd have wanted to smack him into shape. But when I was ten, he was *so* romantic." She prodded gently at the lock for a moment and there was a snick. Jane opened the door. "Don't ever mention to Mel that I know how to do this."

There was a primitive path through the junk in the attic and some fairly fresh-looking cardboard boxes at the far end. The two women gingerly picked their way through and selected two boxes, then paused to examine a few other things. There was a wooden box full of shotgun shells, some shotguns that had been shamefully neglected, and a large old wooden crate full of clothing at the far end of the room. Mostly outdoor stuff. Wellington boots so ancient they were cracked, plaid wool coats, furry hats, lots of gloves and mittens, none of which appeared to have mates. Shelley picked up a pair of old-fashioned jodhpurs with the tips of her fingers. "These might be useable if they were cleaned."

"Perfect for a jaunt to the grocery store," Jane said. "Doorknobs."

"What?"

"A whole box of mixed doorknobs," Jane said, squatting down to look into another wooden box halfway along the path. "Why would anyone collect doorknobs? They're not even interesting or nice ones."

"Oh, look. Croquet sets. Two or three of them," Shelley said. "Let's take one set out and put it up on the lawn. I was a whiz at croquet when I was a kid. I cheated like mad."

They'd made their way to what appeared to be the "sports section" of the attic. There were baseballs with their coverings coming off, bats that had seen better days, a couple of footballs, and a snarl of badminton nets.

"People used to have very different ideas about leisure time," Jane said. "Now when we sit around relaxing together, it's usually in front of a television set or computer screen. It must have been fun to come out here in the summers."

"We better get these boxes down to Livvy. What's that black stuff?"

"Electrical tape?" Jane guessed, glancing down at what looked like a snake nest next to the doorway. "No, it's fabric. Seam binding. How odd. Are you taking the croquet set down?"

"I'll come back with some rags and clean it up a little later," Shelley said.

They closed the attic back up and delivered the boxes to Livvy. The party was showing signs of breaking up. The ladies were tossing back last drinks and looking for their purses. Kitty was being practical and sorting out the gifts and neatly folding the salvageable wrapping paper. Layla was leaning back in a comfortable chair, smiling and looking like she might just fall asleep right there. Eden, who was wearing a loose, colorful tiara of discarded package ribbons, was trying to get the aunts moving along.

"We're going to dinner in a bit. Don't you two need little naps first?" she was asking. Iva's wig appeared to be trying to turn itself around backwards on her head and Marguerite was hanging onto a table as if were the only stable thing in the world. Eden glanced at Jane and grinned. "Those were *very* good champagne cocktails."

Eventually the room cleared. The trophy wives were gathered up by their husbands and taken back to the local motel. The aunts were tucked away in their rooms to sleep it off. Layla hoisted herself out of the chair, staggering only slightly, and went to take a nap, too. Kitty had put away the pretty negligees, slippers, underwear, and more conventional kitchen and bath gifts. Mrs. Hessling was looking extremely sober and very relieved that it was over and was making noises about finding Errol to take her back to the motel. When she'd gone, the only one left was Livvy, who looked tired.

"Get a little rest before dinner," Jane advised her.

"I'll see if Daddy has anything for me to do and if not, I will rest for a while. This is very tiring and must be even more so for you, Jane."

"I don't mind," Jane said. "It's what I came here to do. And most of the hard work was the planning ahead."

Jane stayed behind to tidy up the room a bit more. Shelley had gone to clean up the croquet set. The sounds of the football game had faded as Dwayne's friends had drifted back to the motel to change clothes and clean up for the bachelor party later.

There was only one seemingly untouched glass of champagne left. Mr. Willis came in and started clearing away the last of the plates and Jane made a dive for the drink before he could take it away.

"You did a lovely job, Mr. Willis," she said. "And this really is delicious. No wonder they all had to stagger away."

He nodded his gratitude. "I'm leaving for a while to pick up a few more things and have put salads and dinners in the refrigerator for you and Mrs. Nowack. Will Mr. VanDyne be staying for dinner, too?"

"I don't know. I haven't had much of a chance to speak to him."

"I'll leave enough for him, too, then."

He shimmered off, Jeeves-like, and Jane sipped her champagne in blissful quiet. Which was interrupted a few minutes later by Dwayne Hessling. He looked upset.

"What's wrong?" she asked.

"I've been looking everywhere for you," he said furiously. "Come see."

They met up with Shelley in the main room, loaded down with mallets, balls, and hoops. Sensing something was up, she dumped all of it on a chair and followed Jane and Dwayne to his room.

It had been trashed.

Drawers were pulled out and thrown about, even the empty ones. The contents of his suitcase had been strewn around the room. A bottle of aftershave had been poured all over the bed. In the bathroom, his toothpaste had been squeezed out all over the floor, his shaving gear was in the toilet on top of a wadded-up dress shirt.

"Oh, my gosh!" Shelley whispered.

"What's this about?" Dwayne demanded of Jane.

"I don't know," she said. "When did this happen?"

"While we were all outside," Dwayne said angrily. "I changed my clothes to play football."

"Dwayne, why would anybody do this?" Jane asked.

"Hell if I know."

"Somebody's really mad at you," Shelley said.

"Nobody's got the right to do this to my things. And I want it cleaned up right now."

"Then let's clean it up," Jane said. She'd been sympathetic at first, but his orders, sounding so like Jack Thatcher's, were beginning to annoy her.

"I'm not in charge here, you are. I'm a guest," he sneered.

"You're Mr. Thatcher's guest. Want to ask him to muck around in your toilet?" Jane asked.

"I'm going to find a convenience store to get new toothpaste," he said. "I hope everything is in order when I get back."

He stomped out, leaving Jane and Shelley red-faced and furious. They stared at each other for a long moment. Then Jane said, "I still have one empty room on this hallway. We'll just put his things in there. Dwayne can find other cleaning ladies."

"What a bastard he is," Shelley said.

"It's as if the twerp's been sitting at Jack Thatcher's knee, learning to be an imperious pig of a man," Jane added.

"Jerk. Jerk. Jerk," Shelley muttered, picking up a shirt,

shaking it out, and looking in the rubble for a clothes hanger.

Half an hour later, they closed the door on the room, leaving the tiny window open to air it out, and Jane stuck a note on the door that said: *You're now in the room across the hall.*

Chapter 12

About four, the family and wedding party started gathering in preparation for the rehearsal and dinner afterwards. Running through the wedding itself was a breeze except that the aunts wanted greater roles. What those roles might have been was anybody's guess. They were to be escorted to the first row of chairs on the bride's side as "mother of the bride" substitutes. But at every stage of the proceedings, they kept asking, "What should we be doing now?"

Jane had half a dozen possible sarcastic replies to this query, but restrained herself and kept telling them they were to just sit still and enjoy themselves.

The groom, best man, and groomsmen came in from the side room in good order. Kitty, Layla, and Eden came down the stairs gracefully. If any of them were thinking about Mrs. Crossthwait's deadly descent, they didn't show it. Kitty had made Livvy a really spectacular practice bouquet out of the ribbons and bows from the bridal shower. Livvy, in a pale blue suit she was wearing to dinner, would have made a lovely bride just as she was, ribbon bouquet and all. Jack, escorting her, even looked pleasant and pleased.

The practice only took a few moments to run through. A minibus Jack had hired was waiting at the front door to take the bridal party and families to a very nice restaurant in Chicago, which was why Mr. Willis, as well as Jane and Shelley, were getting a well-deserved break and also the reason they were leaving so early. The travel time plus the dinner would give Jane, Shelley, and Mr. Willis a good five or six hours of blessed quiet.

As the guests started boarding the bus, Jane caught a glimpse of Uncle Joe in a fairly decent suit and tie. "Is he going along?" she whispered to Shelley.

"I can't imagine why he'd be invited," Shelley replied. "He's hired help like us, only of longer duration."

But Uncle Joe got on the bus.

As Eden went back in the lodge for something she'd forgotten, Jane waylaid her. "Eden, why's Uncle Joe included?" she asked bluntly.

Eden looked a bit confused. "Why, because he's part of the family. Didn't you know that?"

"What part, exactly?" Jane asked.

"He's Jack's brother. Illegitimate, of course. Older half-brother, actually, to Jack, Iva, and Marguerite. I thought you knew. That's why he gets to live here for free without doing much work. Have you seen my beaded purse?"

"On the long brown sofa," Jane said, and looked at Shelley with a stunned expression that matched her friend's.

They didn't speak until all the guests were on board and the bus pulled out. Even then, they headed silently for the kitchen. Jane poured them each a cup of coffee and they sat down at the big table in the center of the room.

"Who'd have guessed?" Shelley finally said. "I thought 'Uncle' was just an honorific title. For long service to the family."

"I can't quite get a grip on this," Jane said, peering into her coffee cup as if a revelation might appear there. "Older half-brother, Eden said. So he was born, or at least conceived, before old O. W. even married."

"Eden said the old boy was quite a womanizer."

"Do you suppose his wife knew before she married him?" Jane asked.

"We'll never know, but apparently the rest of the family knows if Eden does," Shelley said. "Uncle Joe really *is* Livvy's uncle."

"It sure accounts for why the aunts are so haughty and cold to him. I thought it was just general snobbiness, but it's very specific snobbiness. The disreputable old guy is their half-brother."

Shelley smiled. "That can't be much fun for them."

"No wonder that nobody makes a point of identifying him as a relative," Jane said. "I wouldn't claim him either."

"But they took him along to dinner as a family member. Wonder if anybody's told the Hesslings?"

"I don't imagine they'd much care."

"Dwayne might," Shelley speculated. "Uncle Joe might come in for some of the family money."

Jane looked up, her eyes widening. "You don't suppose—?"

"That Uncle Joe got the missing money? If there was missing money? Maybe so. But why would he stick around here all these years if he had?"

"Rent free, not much work. The perfect situation for a lazy old man," Jane said. "I wonder if he's always lived here or whether he had a real job and a real life in his younger days and this is just his retirement position."

"I had the impression he'd been a fixture here forever," Shelley said. "But it was only an impression."

They sat quietly for a few minutes, trying to absorb and process this new information about the Thatcher family. Then Shelley brought up Dwayne's room. "Who could have done that to his things, and why?" she asked.

"I suppose it could have been meant as a tacky practical joke. But it seems out of character for the boys—young men—who are here."

"My thoughts exactly. First, they don't look like hoodlums who would find vandalism amusing. They're all a bit on the nerdy side. And secondly, while they might want to do something nasty to Dwayne, they're all so extraordinarily deferential to Jack Thatcher that I don't think they'd consider wrecking the bed and the plumbing on his property. Not a good way to impress a big-deal executive."

"I agree. But a couple of them were in and out of the house while the football game was going on. They had opportunity, if not motive," Jane said.

"But so did nearly everyone," Shelley pointed out. "The ladies at the shower were knocking back the champagne and running back and forth to their bathrooms."

"You think a woman might have done it?"

"I don't see why not. It didn't take any special strength or height. It could have even been the aunts, for that matter."

"Or Jack Thatcher. Or even Uncle Joe," Jane said. "But what was the point? Just to show dislike or contempt?"

"Maybe it was meant as a warning. Stop doing whatever you're doing, Dwayne, or something worse will happen to you."

"But what's he doing besides marrying Livvy?"

Shelley said, "That might be enough. Or it could be something else. We really don't know anything about him except that he's sort of low-rent and is very nasty to anyone close at hand when he's mad."

"I guess about the only person it couldn't have been was Jack Thatcher."

"Why's that?"

"Because all he had to do to stop the wedding was tell Livvy it was off," Jane said.

"You're probably right. And I can't see how Livvy and Dwayne getting married would mean anything to the aunts. So who's left?"

"Bridesmaids and Uncle Joe."

"I vote for Uncle Joe," Shelley said.

"Why? What would his motive be?"

"I don't know. But I'll think of something."

They heard the front door open and footsteps approaching. "Mel? Is that you?" Jane called out.

Mel stepped into the kitchen and headed straight for the refrigerator. "Anything to eat?"

"Mr. Willis left us dinners," Jane said. "Pick whichever plate you like. Where have you been?"

"Just snooping around the grounds," he said, taking the foil off a plate and gazing at the food with disapproval. "Girly-girly stuff. Prissy chicken salad and tiny sandwiches. Is there anything substantial around? I'm starving."

"There probably is, but we don't dare touch it or we

may mess up Mr. Willis's meal plans," Jane said. "There's a McDonald's a couple miles away."

"No, I want real food. A steak and a big baked potato," he said, pouring himself a soft drink and sitting down at the table with them. "Want to go somewhere and see if we can find such a thing?"

"Any other time, I'd snap up that offer," Jane said. "But right now all I want to do is stay here and veg out while there's the chance. Did you know Uncle Joe is the illegitimate half-brother of Jack Thatcher and his sisters?"

"You're kidding!" Mel said. "Come to think of it, there *is* a vague look of an older Jack Thatcher about him. They have the same eyes and hairline."

"Don't you think that's significant?" Jane asked.

"In what way?"

"I'm not sure. It's just odd. They don't seem to have any affection for him. The aunts will hardly speak to him, in fact. But he gets to live here and even go to the rehearsal dinner."

"Every family's got its own rules," Mel said mildly. "This setup isn't half as weird or creepy as a lot I've come across. I had an aunt who invited two of her ex-husbands to her fourth wedding. And they came and had a wonderful time."

"Has anybody mentioned the treasure to you?" Jane asked.

Mel arched an eyebrow and smiled slightly. "The Treasure? Is it a hidden treasure?"

"As a matter of fact, it is," Jane said, suspecting rightly that he was having a joke at her expense. "If it exists at all."

"Okay," Mel said, leaning back in his chair. "Lay it on me."

"We've heard bits of this from several people, but mainly from Eden—"

"The glamorous bridesmaid?"

"I was hoping you wouldn't notice the glamour," Jane said. "Anyhow, according to the aunts, old Oliver Wendell Thatcher was supposed to have a lot more money than showed up when he died. He must have left tons, but they figure there was still a lot more that went missing somewhere."

"Half the families in probate court believe the same thing, Jane," Mel said.

"But in this case, it seems like it could be possible," she replied. "And as Shelley has pointed out, it would have been likely that he was the sort of person who was clever enough to hide money away for his family to keep it from being taxed. Lots of very wealthy people are wary of giving the government more than their fair share of an estate. At least, that's what I hear."

Mel looked rather blank. "Interesting, I guess, but what has it got to do with anything?"

"I think that's why shadowy figures were creeping around in the dark last night. The night Mrs. Crossthwait died," Jane said. "I feel pretty sure one or both of the aunts took down some of those pictures in the main room and took them apart to see if there might be valuable documents hidden in them."

"And accidentally knocked Mrs. Crossthwait down the stairs?"

"Or purposely, maybe," Jane said. "When I was in the main room, someone shined a flashlight in my eyes for a second, then wouldn't respond when I called out. And as I made my way back to my room, somebody brushed by me going in the opposite direction. So there were at least two people roaming around to no good purpose. Maybe more."

"And you think this has to do with the hidden treasure," Mel said. Then he sighed. "Well, I'd feel pretty much of a fool if I ignored this nonsense and it turned out to be relevant. I think I'll drive into town and talk to the local officials again. Yes, in fact, that's a good idea. Cops always know where to get a good meal."

"Oh, Mel. There's something else. Dwayne Hessling's room was trashed this afternoon."

"Trashed?"

"Everything dumped out of his suitcase, clothes deliberately rumpled up, Dwayne's foul aftershave poured all over the bed and toiletries assigned to the toilet."

"Probably his friends' idea of a practical joke."

"We don't think so," Shelley put in. "We think they're ambitious young men who have their imaginations fired up by Dwayne's financial/marital success. They'd be fools not to be on their best behavior while they're here. And Dwayne was furious about it. If he were part of a crowd that ran to that kind of 'joke,' I don't think he'd have been so angry."

Mel had listened seriously. "Okay. You two could be right. But what do you figure the real point was?"

"It looked to me like a threat of some kind. A warning, I think," Jane said. "Do such-and-such and worse things will happen to you. There was a very destructive, nasty feeling in that room."

"And do you figure this has something to do with Mrs. Crossthwait's death, the silly treasure story, or Uncle Joe's birth circumstances as well?"

"You're verging on sarcasm, aren't you?" Jane said.

"Not verging. Wading right in," Mel said.

Jane was tired and cranky. But she knew better than to say anything she'd later regret. "We're just telling you what we know and think that the local police might not have come across. If you want to pass it along, fine. If you don't, that's okay, too."

Mel was more chastised by this approach than he would have been if she'd been nasty. "Okay. I see your point. I'll go hunt down Officer Smith and pass this along while I try to find out what else he might know. Sure you don't want to come along?"

"No, I like prissy chicken salad. The prissier the better," Jane said.

Chapter 13

Mel ended up having dinner with Officer John Smith at an old roadhouse that didn't even have a sign in front. It was strictly a neighborhood male hangout and specialized in excellent chicken fried steak and mediocre beer.

"I'd be glad for the company," Smith said when Mel offered to treat him to dinner. "My wife's visiting her mother with the kids and I'm a lousy cook. Listen, if you'd like, let me invite somebody else along, too."

"Sure," Mel had said.

Smith made a phone call and they set out for the roadhouse. "I've asked Gus Ambler to meet us. He's a good man who was county sheriff for a dog's age. If there's any background on the lodge that would help us, Ambler'll know all about it."

Gus Ambler looked like a tough, fat little fighting cock. What little hair he still had was short and white, but he had the coloring of a once-redhead. Mel knew from what Smith had said that Ambler had to be in his seventies, maybe early eighties, but he looked like a "rode-hard-and-put-away-wet" fifty. He couldn't have been more than five feet tall and walked with the belligerent, rolling gait of an old sailor.

Ambler was already at the roadhouse and halfway through his first beer when Mel and Smith arrived. Smith performed the introductions and Mel said, "If you'd ever arrested me, I'd have been scared spitless."

Ambler preened. "And you'da been right, boy! I had 'em shaking in their boots in my day. So what are you boys up to that you need to talk to an old geezer like me?"

"You heard about the death at the Thatchers' lodge?" Smith asked.

"I hear about everything, boy. Got a perp yet?"

"Nope," Smith said. "But we're pretty sure it was someone in the house. Thought you might tell us a bit about the lodge and the Thatchers."

Ambler glared at Mel. "And what's your place in this?"

"I'm just a guest. A friend of mine is in charge of planning the wedding that's going on tomorrow and I'm watching out for her interests. Besides, I'm curious."

"And he's a good cop, too," Smith put in. He reeled off a list of some of the difficult cases Mel had been responsible for solving.

"How'd you know that?" Mel asked.

Smith looked surprised. "I checked you out. Just like I did everybody. Anybody can create a fake ID these days. Wouldn't you have done the same?"

Mel grinned. "Exactly the same."

"So you're one of us," Ambler said. While they were studying the menus, a waste of time since they were all going to have the famous chicken fried steak anyway, Ambler ran through a few of the cases he'd been involved in.

They went clear back to Prohibition days when he was just a kid, hanging out with his uncle, who'd been a deputy.

Mel loved nothing better than to sit around with a tough old cop telling stories of the good old days, but Smith had apparently heard the stories before and gently guided the elderly man back to what he knew of the lodge.

"It was a monastery to start with. I guess you knew that. Bunch of sissy boys from back East came out here in long brown dresses with a rich guy who musta thought they could pray his way into heaven," Ambler said.

A tired-looking waitress came by and slammed three beers on the table and took their orders.

"Anyhow," Ambler went on, "the rich guy died after they'd been here a couple o' years and the money ran out. I guess he figured he didn't need the prayers after he was dead so he didn't leave them any money to get along on. The monks tried growing vegetables and keeping bees and weaving stuff and whatnot, even turned a hand at making soap for a while, but they gave up and sold the place to O. W. Thatcher. That musta been in about 1932 or '33. Bad times, those were. But O. W. didn't seem to be hurting for money like the rest of us. He was a young man then, but ran his dad's company selling little junky stuff like folding rulers and toothpick holders and such. Can't imagine how he made a dime on toothpick holders, being as most of us then couldn't even afford toothpicks . . ."

Mel had the feeling this story might not ever really get off the ground. Smith apparently did, too. "So did O. W. spend a lot of time here?"

"Not at first. Only hunting season. He'd come down here with a bunch of his Chicago cronies and man, were they ever a terror! Drinking like fish, driving around the countryside like maniacs, picking off people's cats and dogs with their rifles."

"Not very welcome in the neighborhood, then?" Mel asked.

"Not welcome a'tall. No, sirree. But it got better after a bit. O. W. got married, had a couple kids, started bringing friends' families down instead of his drinking buddies. By that time, the money situation had eased up and there was less resentment of him on that account, too."

"Was the guy they call 'Uncle Joe' part of the family?" Mel asked.

"Lordy, no! He was O. W.'s bastard kid. The wife probably wouldn't have heard of having him around underfoot. Wasn't until she died when the other kids were in their teens that O. W. dragged Joe into the family. And he was a wild one. In all kinds of trouble when he got here, but then the war came and he went off. And he came back different."

"Different in what way?"

"Not wild, for one thing. Quiet-like and always sort of cranky. People said he had some kind of injury, but nobody seemed to know just what. Nothing showed. He didn't limp or have a deaf ear or anything like that. Rumor was that he had some shrapnel in his head, but I don't know that it was true. People'll make up what they need to think."

The waitress brought their food, which was wonderful, and they ate in silence for a while. Eventually Ambler burped heartily and went on. "Anyhow, O. W. kept Joe on at the lodge. Guess he felt he owed the boy something, being as he wasn't quite fit to go out in the world. And I gotta give Joe credit. When O. W. got old and pretty dotty,

Joe was the one who took care of him. O. W. spent a lot of his later years at the lodge.''

''So they got along well?'' Mel asked.

''Hell, no! Neither one of them was fit company for a polecat, but they rubbed along okay. Joe took him back and forth to Chicago to doctors. Bitched the whole time about it, but did it. O. W. was always complaining that Joe was starving him to death, but he kept gaining weight until the last stroke when Joe couldn't handle him anymore and was forced to put him in a nursing home.''

''Did O. W. leave Joe anything?''

''Not so's you'd notice. But Joe's kind of a nut about his privacy. He never said. And it was one of those trust things that don't go through probate and become public record, so nobody could check. Joe might have got a fortune, but you'd never know. He's as tight and stingy as O. W. was. Even in the old days, when the hard drinkers were down here, word was they had to bring their own booze. O. W. liked the company, but wouldn't pay for their guzzling.''

''Did Jack and his sisters visit much?'' Mel asked.

''It went in spells. The girls would get hard-up or want a trip to Europe and they'd make up to the old man. Jack came down a lot, but it was always about business,'' Ambler said. ''The old man insisted on keeping his finger in the pie.''

''How do you know this?'' Mel asked mildly.

Gus Ambler laughed. ''Good detectin'. Actually, my late wife sometimes helped at the lodge. Mucked out the place for spring cleaning. Did a little darning and ironing and such. Every time she did canning or baking, she made extra for O. W. and Joe. Said she felt sorry for both of them with no women to look after them."

The waitress came back for their plates, all three of which looked like they'd been licked clean. "Got any of that rhubarb pie?" Gus Ambler asked.

"You don't need no pie, Gus," she said.

"Just a sociable piece to eat with my friends. Three of 'em," he said, ignoring her assessment of his figure.

Mel didn't want to make a fool of himself asking about the treasure, but he had to at least make a stab at the subject. He'd blame it on Jane. "My friend Mrs. Jeffry," he said, "the one who's managing the wedding, says a couple people there have mentioned a treasure."

He expected the tough old sheriff to laugh himself silly and was astonished when Gus said mildly, "Yeah, everybody knows about that."

"You mean there is one?" Mel asked.

Ambler made an expansive "I dunno" gesture. "I meant everybody's heard the story. Don't know if it's true. It wouldn't have been so strange if O. W. had left his money and property to the three legitimate kids and left something else to Joe."

"But if Joe had secretly inherited a lot, why would he go on living in the lodge?" Officer Smith asked. He'd been quiet all through dinner, probably because he was busy eating the only decent meal he'd had since his wife left town.

"I reckon it's because it's the only place he knows," Gus Ambler said. "He's got his television and radio, his hunting magazines and no ambition or interest in much of anything. And where could he go where he'd have the same privacy?"

"What will he do when the lodge is torn down this summer?" Mel asked.

"I asked him that when I ran into him at Wanda's a week or two ago," John said. "It was a mistake. He told me to mind my own business and he'd go wherever he damn well pleased."

Ambler nodded. "Pretty much the same reaction I got when I tried to talk to him about it."

"So it's possible he does have the means of setting himself up someplace else?" Mel asked.

"So he says," Ambler said, looking around for the waitress. "Where's that pie, honey?" he yelled across the room when he caught her eye.

"I think he does have something hidden," John Smith volunteered. "We get a lot of calls from him. Prowlers, peeping Toms, trespassers. Could be his imagination, since we never find anyone. Or it could be that he's protecting something valuable."

"Or something he reckons is valuable," Ambler added.

"What do you mean?" Mel asked.

"Well, toward the end of O. W.'s days, he got real ambitious. Had some builders in. Out-of-town builders, mind you. So they couldn't gossip about what they were doing. Had a couple rooms painted and fixed up. A wall torn out and another put up. Changed the locks. Sent out a couple of those moth-eaten old animal heads to a taxidermist. Replaced the doorknobs so they were all the same, had some kind of work done on the old well. Again, by outsiders. Patched up the roof and I don't know what all . . ."

"Your wife reported this?" Mel said with a grin.

"She watched like a hawk. Thought it was out of character. Anyway, the work was almost done when O. W. had the first stroke. It was a pretty bad one. Twisted up his face, made him lame, and got him pretty nutsy. He'd wander off at night. Only thing that saved him was that he made such a racket with his walker that Joe always heard him. Anyhow, the thing I've always wondered was this: if he was having this work done to hide something, and he had the first stroke before he could tell Joe what he was up to, he might have forgotten it. He forgot that he needed to go in a bathroom to pee indoors and even forgot his own name half the time."

The pie finally arrived and was every bit as good as the chicken fried steak. Gus Ambler ate with relish for a few minutes, then asked Mel, "So how do you figure this has anything to do with that woman being murdered?"

"I doubt that it does," Mel said honestly. He turned to John Smith and asked, "How are you getting along on finding out about the rest of the people who were there?"

"Finding out a lot," Smith said. "But none of it seems especially relevant. That Dwayne guy that Livvy's marrying has a teenage shoplifting record. It should have been expunged years ago, but was still on the books by accident. His mother is clean as a whistle and the brother had a speeding ticket two years ago."

"Where's he work? Dwayne, I mean?" Mel asked.

"He's the junior-most vice president in a little branch of a big mortgage company. Paid with a title instead of money like those outfits do people," Smith said.

"No financial hanky-panky?" Gus Ambler asked.

"Can't be sure exactly. His boss didn't have much to say about him," Smith replied. "I got the impression he didn't much like the boy, but had no specific criticism he wanted to talk about. The boss is a pretty small cog himself and wouldn't risk causing trouble for himself. He did say that Dwayne was winding up his work and moving to his new wife's company after the wedding."

"What about the victim?" Ambler asked. "That's the place to start."

"Harmless, annoying old woman. The local police where she lived found paperwork about some kind of fight she was having with the I.R.S. and the Social Security people. Apparently there's a discrepancy between what she paid in her self-employment taxes and what she was trying to get from Social Security. Wads of paperwork from both agencies and her accountant. But I can't see that it has anything to do with her death. We talked to the accountant. The only thing that came out of it is that he's also the accountant for one of the bridesmaids' fathers. Eden Matthews. The curvy one."

"I know which one she is," Mel said with a grin.

"It seems like simple coincidence," Smith said. "I can't see a way it would be connected. The accountant also said that a couple of years ago Mrs. Crossthwait tried to start some sewing classes. Rented sewing machines and a room at a community center. It didn't fly and that's when her tax troubles started. His wife, out of compassion, signed up and said Crossthwait was so critical and nasty to the students that half of them never came back. He had deposit slips showing those who had signed up and one of them was a Hessling, possibly the groom's mother, though the deposit slip didn't give a first name."

"Did she stick out the course?" Mel asked.

"No way the accountant could tell. Only two of them tried, unsuccessfully, to get their money back. The rest just didn't come back," Smith said.

"Seems unlikely that Mrs. Hessling would harbor a grudge for years over a sewing class. Enough of a grudge to kill the teacher," Mel said. "Not to mention that it might not even be the same person."

Smith shrugged. "Closer to impossible. Mrs. Crossthwait also kept a big old scrapbook of wedding pictures of all the brides she'd sewed for. One of the earliest was Jack Thatcher's sister Marguerite. But it was eons ago."

"What about the other people who were in the house the night she died?" Ambler asked.

"Nothing much. No police or legal records on the bridesmaids. The florist is weird as hell, but hasn't stepped outside the law as far as we know. The caterer had to sue someone two years ago to get his bill paid, otherwise nothing else on him."

Mel asked, "And Uncle Joe, who often sees or imagines prowlers, didn't report any that night?"

"Not a peep from him that night," Smith confirmed.

"Sounds to me like you've got a mess on your hands," Ambler said gruffly. "Any chance the woman who died wasn't the intended victim?"

"Anything's possible, but it doesn't seem very likely," Smith said. "Want the last of my pie? I'm stuffed."

As Mel and Smith headed back to the police station, Mel said, "I'm glad you asked Gus Ambler along. He's a good ol' boy, isn't he?"

"He was . . . tonight," Smith said, smiling.

"What do you mean?" Mel asked, loosening his belt a notch and wondering how he'd ever be able to eat again after his massive dinner.

"Just that he was doing his 'country cop' act. After he

retired and his wife had passed away, he got bored. So he got himself into Harvard and took a law degree."

"You're kidding!"

"Not a bit. And get this—he drives a hundred miles once a week to teach art appreciation to some little college he's got a soft spot for. Doesn't even charge them."

Mel was quiet for a couple miles, brooding unhappily over his misperception of the man. Finally, he said, "I think I've been had."

"Everybody who's run into Gus feels that way. Eventually."

❖

Chapter 14

When Jane and Shelley had finished their dinner, they went to Mrs. Crossthwait's room and started the sad job of gathering up and packing her things. She had, it appeared, come with everything she could possibly have needed and much more besides. There were tidy boxes of bobbins, buttons, needles, and a large, well-organized case with thread of every weight and color imaginable. There was a full kit of tiny repair tools, belts, and screws for the sewing machine.

"I've always wanted to have an entire collection of . . . something," Shelley said. "This comes as close as anything I've ever seen. What's this thing?" she asked, holding up a little gadget.

Jane glanced at it. "I think it goes with the sewing machine. A thing for making ruffles, maybe? I'll bet there's a case that holds all those things. Here. This green plastic carton. See? Little compartments everything fits into."

"She really knew her stuff, didn't she?" Shelley said. "At least she had all the equipment. Poor old thing. I wonder who'll get all this."

"I hope it's somebody who appreciates it. I guess her church friends will have to decide what to do with her things if she doesn't have family. Shelley, what do you suppose she was doing anywhere near the stairs in the middle of the night?"

"Going down for a midnight snack?"

"I don't think she had a flashlight," Jane said. "At least, I didn't notice one on the steps or the floor. Of course, it might have rolled under a sofa or chair."

"She might have been meeting someone," Shelley suggested.

Jane shook her head. "Not in her jammies. Not a woman of her generation. She'd have stayed dressed if she had plans to see someone, I think."

"Maybe she just heard an alarming noise and went to investigate."

"Last night was nothing *but* alarming noises, Shelley. All that lightning and thunder. And being as she was already spooked about auras, and a tad deaf on top of it, I don't think she'd have willingly gone prowling around without a flashlight and probably a weapon like some sharp scissors."

"Okay, I'm out of suggestions. Have you got any?"

"Nope," Jane said, looking for the box where the packet of cherry pink seam binding must have belonged. "What if someone told her there was something wrong and we had to get out of the house?"

"Like a fire?"

"Yes. A fire. Exactly. As slowly as she moved, she'd have probably been terrified of being in a burning building. Well, so would I, come to that. Or maybe somebody told her there was a big limb hanging over her room that could crash down on the house at any moment."

Shelley sat down on the edge of the bed. "You may have something there. Scaring her about some danger is about the only reason I can imagine that would get her out of her room, in the dark, in her nightwear."

Jane had found the box of hem tapes and seam bindings and put the leftover packet into it. She had another one she'd found on the floor as well. "Shelley, remember in the attic there was a wad of black seam binding?"

"Vaguely."

"I just remembered something. It wasn't old and dusty. And here's another packet of black that's only got a few inches left."

Jane crossed the landing to the attic, opened the door, and glanced around. After tripping over the box of door-knobs, she found the tape. "Here it is," she said as Shelley trailed in behind her. "And look at the end of the tape in the packet and this end of the stuff on the floor."

"They match. It's a jagged cut. But why would Mrs. Crossthwait have cut off a huge section and thrown it away in here? She had a big wastebasket in her room."

"Because she didn't do it. Someone else did."

"I don't get it, Jane. What are you talking about?"

"My guess is that somebody lifted the packet during the evening, strung it across one of the steps after the lights went out, and slipped what remained back into Mrs. Crossthwait's belongings sometime later."

Shelley's eyes widened. "To make quite certain she tripped on the stairs, even if the push didn't do it!"

"Right. And then the person untied the seam binding—see where it's crinkled from being tied? And pitched it in the attic, thinking nobody would go in there, and if they did, it would just be more junk if it were noticed at all."

"That's really diabolical," Shelley said. "But how does it help?"

"I don't know. Except it proves that Mrs. Crossthwait's death was planned. It wasn't a spur of the moment thing."

Shelley shivered. "Euwww. I don't like this at all. What a horrible scenario!"

Jane looked down at the tangle of binding. "I don't imagine this stuff would hold fingerprints, would it?"

"Jane, it's getting dark and I don't like us being up here alone. Leave the seam binding here and let's finish packing things up and we can go sit in the kitchen until Mel comes back. I suddenly don't much enjoy our solitude. I wish there were someone else around. Preferably a man. With a gun."

They went back to Mrs. Crossthwait's room. "Speaking of men, I haven't seen Larkspur for ages," Jane said, picking up an armload of boxes full of sewing notions. "He didn't say anything about leaving, did he?"

"Not to me. Where are we going with this stuff?"

"To her car. If we load everything into it, whoever comes to fetch it will have all her belongings."

It took a couple trips, but they got everything except the sewing machine into the car; Jane planned to ask one of the strong young men to carry it out later. Jane put Mrs. Crossthwait's purse out of sight under the front seat, locked the Jeep, and pocketed the keys.

They headed for the kitchen to make some fresh coffee and found Larkspur leaning into the fridge, rummaging for sustenance.

"Where have you been?" Jane asked. "I was starting to worry about you."

He continued to search the fridge. "Just here and there. I found some fabulous columbines back behind Uncle Joe's rabbit hutch of a house. They're not in bloom and might get really doggy flowers, but the foliage is magnificent. And there's a fern there that I can't identify."

"But no treasure?" Jane asked.

He whirled around, bumping his head smartly on the egg tray on the door. "Treasure?" he asked with exaggerated innocence.

"That's what you're really looking for, isn't it?" Shelley said. "How did you happen to hear about it?"

Larkspur took Mel's dinner plate out of the refrigerator. "May I have this, my dears?" At Jane's nod, he sat down at the table and took the foil off the plate. "Oh, lovely chicken salad. Divine. How *did* I hear about the treasure? Oh, yes. I mentioned to a customer that I was doing a wedding at a hunting lodge and was rather wondering what would complement deer antlers. The customer asked where the lodge was and he said he'd once lived somewhere nearby and told me about the treasure."

"Did he say what the nature of it was?"

"No, just that everybody in town believed there was something hidden in the lodge or the grounds that was extremely valuable."

"Who was this person?" Jane asked.

Larkspur made a flapping motion with both hands. "My dear, how could I possibly remember? I have absolute flocks of people in and out of the shop and it was months and months ago. Why? Does it matter who it was?"

"I guess not," Jane said. "Since it seems to be such a common rumor."

"Rumor? Are you really sure of that?" Larkspur asked.

"I'm not sure of anything except that I want this wedding to be over," Jane said. "So I can go home and sink back into being an antisocial slob."

"Testy, testy, my dear. And I'm absolutely certain you're never a slob. Antisocial perhaps on occasion, everybody's entitled to that, but not a slob. Where has your handsome detective friend gone?"

"Out to dinner. That's his that you're eating."

"Will he mind?" Larkspur asked, tucking into the chicken salad as if afraid someone might take it away from him.

"No, he's gone out and gotten a social life. Well, a professional social life," Jane said. "Maybe that's him now," she said at the sound of a door opening.

But it was Mr. Willis with a vast tray of ham and egg rolls, which he popped into the oven, but didn't turn the heat on yet. He was back in a moment with grocery bags full of beer, pretzels, chips, and dips.

"You shouldn't have," Larkspur simpered.

Mr. Willis looked down his stubby nose. "They're not for you. They're for the bachelor party. The young men won't care that it's not gourmet food."

"The wedding party isn't back from dinner yet, are they?" Jane said, glancing at her watch.

"Not yet. But the beer has to chill."

"Mr. Willis, have you heard anything about a treasure hidden in the lodge?" Shelley asked as he started stacking beer cans in the refrigerator.

"Who hasn't?" he asked over his shoulder. "It's not in the pantry. That's all I can tell you."

"You searched?" Jane asked.

"Who wouldn't?" he asked. "But I think it's foolish. I've worked in two restaurants that were in old houses that were supposed to have hidden treasures. I was there when one of them was discovered."

"What was it?" Larkspur inquired.

"A stack of old stock certificates for a defunct mining company. Hidden in the wall of an old pocket door. The owner had them framed as decorations for the walls and renamed the restaurant the Miner's Dream."

"What's a pocket door?" Shelley asked.

"The kind of door that slides into a thick wall," Jane said.

"Are there any here?"

"No," Larkspur answered with certainty. "And there's nothing in or around the well or the crawl space under the house."

"You grubbed around under the house?" Jane asked.

"Just by poking a flashlight into holes in the foundation. If there's anything here, I imagine the wrecking crew will get it."

"Is that how it works when something's torn down?" Shelley asked.

"I think so. That's how those pricey salvage companies get all the plaster and marble ornamentation to sell to suburbanites with more money than taste."

Shelley bridled. "I just happen to have a section of egg and dart molding from the outside of an old office building in my front garden."

Larkspur wasn't embarrassed. "But you, my darling,

are the exception that proves the rule. I must go set up the flowers for the bachelor party."

As he left, Shelley whispered, "Aren't flowers for a bachelor party a bit much?"

"They're very macho flower arrangements," Jane replied. "Yucca leaves and those big obscene red plastic-looking flowers with the white thing sticking up out of them. He's tossing them in for free as a bit of a vulgar joke."

Jane was desperately eager for Mel to return so she and Shelley could pick his brain about anything he might have learned. But he came back to the lodge looking a bit green around the gills and was only moments ahead of the minibus with the wedding party coming back from dinner in Chicago. Jane reluctantly let him go to his room to nap off his dinner and threw herself back into her "hired hostess" role. Mr. Willis rushed the beer and grocery store snacks to the room where the bridal shower had been held earlier in the day, and Jane helped him put out wines, sherries, and elegant little nibbles in the main room for any guests who might be settling in there.

Shelley breezed through with an armload of coats she'd relieved the aunts and the bridesmaids of, and whispered, "Just think, Jane, it's eleven o'clock. By this time tomorrow, we'll all be home and this will be but a pleasant memory."

"Yeah, right. If we all survive until tomorrow night," Jane muttered, polishing a water spot off a sherry glass with the tail of her blouse.

❖

Chapter 15

The bachelor party sputtered into action. The group consisted of Dwayne, his brother, his groomsmen, Jack Thatcher, and a couple of the older man's business associates. Uncle Joe wasn't there. Jane hadn't handled the invitations, so she didn't know if Joe's absence was because Jack didn't want him there or Joe had refused to come. The young men, determined to impress their important elders, were awkward and gauche in their efforts to behave. The older men were bored senseless. Jane peeked in the door a couple times and on each occasion the two groups were keeping their distance.

Jane and Shelley took over a pair of chairs just outside the room, in case Jane were to be needed. "What loads of fun they seem to be having," Shelley said sarcastically.

"Poor things," Jane said.

"Which ones?"

"All of them. There's nothing worse than an obligatory festivity."

"I don't know—I think you're forgetting childbirth, tax

audits, frozen pipes, flat tires downtown during rush hour, college tuition . . ."

Jane put up her hand. "Okay, okay."

Several of the women were also sitting around in the main room, but keeping their distance from Jane and Shelley. Whether by design or accident was questionable. The aunts were fiddling with the tuner on the old upright radio in the far corner. Possibly, Jane thought, to get a weather report. There were faint rumbles of thunder in the distance and Jane devoutly hoped there wouldn't be a repeat of the previous night's storms. There was still the possibility of having to hold the wedding in the dark.

Eden had commandeered the best lamp and had a vast array of fingernail cosmetics on a table. There were half a dozen files and buffers, a kaleidoscope of bottles of colored polishes, and a selection of bottles of mysterious liquids. Kitty and Layla were finishing up yet another jigsaw puzzle on a big, hoof-footed coffee table by the fireplace.

Mrs. Hessling wasn't among them. She'd come back with everybody else on the minibus, but had pleaded weariness and Errol had taken her back to the motel. Nor was Livvy anywhere in sight. Jane had no idea where the bride might have gone, but kept reminding herself that she was the wedding planner, not the girl's mother, and it was none of her business where Livvy spent the evening before her Big Day.

A few minutes after Jane and Shelley settled in, Mel reappeared, rested but a bit bleary. "What's going on?" he asked.

"Not much," Jane said. "A floundering bachelor party. So tell us what you learned this evening."

Mel briefly reviewed his dinner with John Smith and

Gus Ambler, hitting all the high points. The monks, the drunken hunting parties, the ascent (or descent, depending on how you looked at it) into domesticity, and Uncle Joe's arrival and Gus's perception of him as a wild boy who went off to war and came back vaguely damaged. He repeated what Gus had said about O. W. being so tightfisted all his life and pretty dotty at the end.

"But he gave Joe full credit for taking good care of his father as long as he could. Not with much good grace, however."

"Did you mention the treasure rumor?" Jane asked.

"I did, and to my surprise, he didn't fall down laughing at a city slicker suggesting it."

"So he thinks there was one?"

"He didn't go that far. Only allowed as how it was barely possible." Mel went on to explain about the renovations done at the end of O. W.'s life and his secrecy about just what was being done to the house and why.

"So he could have slipped in a secret passage or hidden something in a wall?" Jane asked.

Mel looked highly skeptical. "You've been reading old gothic novels again, haven't you?"

"I'm serious, Mel. Why would anybody have new walls put in and hire an out-of-area firm to do it unless there was a secret room he didn't want the locals to know about?"

"Maybe there weren't local carpenters he thought were any good," Mel said. "And maybe he was just getting a bit paranoid. He was elderly and might have already been having little strokes that didn't make a physical difference, but altered his mental attitude."

Shelley said, "I don't see how any of this could possibly have to do with Mrs. Crossthwait's death. Unless she discovered something in the lodge that Uncle Joe didn't want her to talk about."

Jane shook her head. "Mrs. Crossthwait didn't strike me as a very observant person. And I can't see her roaming around looking the place over. How would she have even suspected there was a treasure?"

"Narcissus knew," Mel said.

"You mean Larkspur," Jane said. "That's true. And he had no connection with this place until the wedding was planned."

"Could that be why she was so slow with the dresses?" Shelley speculated. "So she would be invited out here? I don't think the dressmaker is normally invited to the wedding."

Jane's eyes widened. "You could be onto something there. Livvy picked her because she heard Mrs. Crossthwait had an excellent reputation, but that couldn't have been true unless she got the dresses for other people done in a timely manner. If Larkspur had heard the rumor of something valuable hidden here, Mrs. Crossthwait could have just as well heard it, too."

"But I don't think, even if this is all true, that Uncle Joe is the only suspect," Shelley said. "Suppose . . . suppose the treasure, if it exists, is something big and obvious?"

"Like what?" Jane asked.

"I don't know. But just as an example, maybe one of these big pieces of furniture is incredibly valuable. Made by someone terribly famous, or with a long exotic history of being in the room where the tsar and his family were assassinated. Don't roll your eyes that way, Jane. I'm just making up examples."

"Go on," Jane said, stifling a smile.

"Okay, so if it's something that would be obvious if it went missing, anybody in the family might know, but couldn't just tuck it under their arm and trot off with it. They'd want to wait until Uncle Joe was out of here and the place was about to be torn down, then they'd run up here with a pickup truck and two strong moving men and snaffle the thing."

Since neither Jane nor Mel was openly laughing at her yet, Shelley went on. "So we know very little about Mrs. Crossthwait's background, but people sometimes have weird little pockets of knowledge. Like you, Jane, and that particular skill of yours." Shelley made a gesture of wiggling a seam ripper in a lock.

"What's that?" Mel asked.

"Shelley's just kidding, Mel," Jane said a bit too forcefully.

"So Mrs. Crossthwait says to someone in the family, 'My goodness, that wagon in the yard outside looks just like the tumbril that took Marie Antoinette to the guillotine.' And if that person has been waiting quietly for years to make off with the wagon, knowing the same thing, Mrs. Crossthwait is suddenly, and stupidly, a big threat to them."

"That surely eliminates the aunts, doesn't it?" Jane asked. "It seems that they're still trying to find out what and where the treasure is."

Shelley nodded. "But only if we're right that they were the ones roaming around last night stealing pictures and taking them apart."

"The most likely person to know, next to Uncle Joe, is Jack Thatcher," Jane said. "He's spent the most time here."

"Or Livvy herself," Shelley said. "She's probably had

an excellent education. Even if all she wanted to study was business, I'm sure Jack expected her to have all the social graces. Know about history and art and such."

Mel had been listening to this conversation without contributing. Now he did. "Ladies, this is all nuts. You're letting your imaginations run away with you. And it's not your problem or even mine. Just as long as you're careful to keep yourselves safe for another few hours, it's up to John Smith to figure it all out. And it might not have even been murder, come to that."

"But what about the 'push' marks on Mrs. Crossthwait?" Jane said.

Mel shrugged. "Good point, but maybe when she tumbled down the stairs, she fell on something that made that sort of marks."

"Mel, your imagination is as vivid as ours are," Jane said. "What else could have made them? Falling against the outstretched hand of a marble statue? There aren't any of those around."

Mel looked embarrassed. "Okay, okay. But maybe someone else was roaming around in the dark, ran into her, and just out of fright and alarm, gave her a shove? Not even knowing who she was."

"It won't play, Mel," Jane said. "First of all, she wouldn't have been anywhere near the stairs in the dark without having been deliberately lured out of her room. She was already afraid of going up and down those stairs in full daylight."

"I learned a couple things from John Smith, too," Mel said. "Apparently she made Marguerite Rowe's wedding dress sometime back in the Dark Ages."

"She claimed that, and Marguerite brushed her off," Jane said.

"She also has an accountant in common with Eden's father."

"What could that mean?" Jane asked.

"Almost certainly nothing," Mel said. "And she once had a sewing class that a Mrs. Hessling attended."

"You're just a wealth of information," Jane said. "But how does any of it help?"

"I'm not claiming it helps. Just reporting."

"What about Dwayne? Did they find out anything about him?" Jane asked.

Mel decided the teenaged shoplifting charge wasn't something he should discuss. "Not much. His boss was pretty closed-mouth about him. Whether he was concealing something the company didn't want talked about or he simply doesn't like the kid very well wasn't clear. He said Dwayne was going to work for Livvy's father and didn't express any regret at losing him."

Shelley suddenly gasped.

"What's wrong?" Jane asked.

"The seam binding! We forgot to tell Mel about the seam binding!"

Jane nearly slapped her own forehead. "How could we forget!" She explained to him about the fresh, non-dusty seam binding they'd found in the attic while he was out to dinner and their theory that it had been tied across the stairway to make quite certain Mrs. Crossthwait would take a serious tumble.

"Where is it now?" he asked in a low voice.

"I think we left it in the attic," Shelley said.

"You haven't mentioned this to anyone else, have you?" Mel asked.

"Of course not," Jane said.

"Then don't. Stay here. I'm going to call Smith and have him take a look."

He got up and strolled away with seeming casualness.

"He's taking us seriously for once," Jane said with surprise.

"What are you two plotting?" Eden Matthews said from behind Jane. Neither she nor Shelley had seen her approach and Jane wondered if she'd overheard any of their conversation.

"Nothing much," Jane said. "Just chatting about the plans for tomorrow."

Eden took the chair Mel had been sitting in. She was still in her dinner dress, a slinky black number with a plunging neckline and what looked like a real diamond brooch to draw the eye to the extent of the plunge. She really was a gorgeous, voluptuous woman. "Your boyfriend is very good-looking," she said to Jane.

"I think so, too," Jane said.

"Where's he gone?"

"I'm not sure. He didn't say." Jane wondered fleetingly whether Eden was really asking if he'd gone to bed and intended to pursue him there. Rather than let herself follow this line of thought, she asked, "How was the rehearsal dinner?"

"Wonderful. Excellent food. Nice surroundings, but not the best of company, I have to admit. Dwayne was in a bit of a rage about his room being messed up. He couldn't quit complaining about it. Didn't make for scintillating conversation."

"That's too bad," Shelley said. "Was he blaming anyone in particular?"

"Oh, just about everybody in turn. Not blatantly enough for anyone to justify taking offense—quite. But he was very annoying. Set everyone's teeth on edge."

"What does he do for a living?" Shelley asked.

"I have the impression he's been a very insignificant clerk in a very large mortgage company. Researches deeds or something boring like that. But he's coming into the family firm when he and Livvy get back from their honeymoon. I can't imagine what he can contribute."

"Besides sons for Livvy?" Shelley said.

Eden grinned. "It probably *is* just a ploy to keep him close at hand and under Jack's control. I never thought about it that way, but you're probably right. Keeps him under Jack's watchful eye and prevents him from advancing elsewhere and having a job if he even thinks about getting out of the marriage eventually. That's very perceptive of you."

"Who do you think messed up his room?" Jane asked, inadvertently cutting short Shelley's appreciation of the compliment.

"I'd have done it if I'd thought of it, just to provide an irritant," Eden said with a wicked smile. "But I didn't. I don't know. His own chums are the best possibility. They're all a tad low-rent, don't you think? And it's such a male thing."

"Actually, I'd guess they're all pretty ambitious," Shelley replied. "They're obviously in awe of Jack Thatcher and his successful friends. I think some of them harbor the illusion that one of these rich businessmen will recognize their sterling qualities and pluck them out of the abyss of lower management."

Eden stared at Shelley for a moment with a look of surprise. "Yes. Yes, I can see that. But who would that leave? Not me. Not you two. You don't want anything messing up the wedding."

"The aunts?" Jane suggested.

Eden shook her head. "No, they live for tidiness. Both of them have three-times-a-week cleaning ladies. And besides, why would they want to make him miserable?"

"Maybe just because they don't approve of him marrying Livvy," Jane said, thinking this was pretty thin reasoning, but unable to come up with anything else.

Eden stirred in her chair and yawned. "I guess we'll never know. I'm giving it up for the night. Have to get my beauty sleep."

Jane and Shelley sat silently watching her leave. Then Shelley said, "It's odd. Nobody seems to have much affection for Dwayne. Not even his own mother. And if Livvy is passionate about him, she certainly doesn't show it."

"And at least one person seems to actively dislike him. The one who wrecked his belongings," Jane said. After another few minutes of thought, she added, "And it's very possible that someone in this wedding party is capable of murder. If I were Dwayne, I'd be worried. In fact, I *am* worried."

Chapter 16

Uncle Joe turned up about ten minutes before the bachelor party ended. He wandered into the side room where it was being held and wandered back out a moment later with a cold beer in one hand and a fistful of pretzels in the other. Jane wondered if he'd appeared just to show he was entitled to attend, but chose not to participate. Or had he just wanted a free beer? He sat down near Shelley and Jane, but not close enough to encourage conversation. Jane nodded at him politely and he nodded back.

Aunt Iva and Aunt Marguerite had been seated at the far end of the room, sipping sherry and holding an animated, but whispered chat, and now rose and approached Jane and Shelley. "What is the schedule for tomorrow?" Iva asked.

"Breakfast from seven to eight. A light lunch at twelve and the wedding itself at two," Jane said. She'd prepared and handed out this information, nicely printed out on pink card stock, to all the family members as they arrived, but apparently Iva and Marguerite had lost theirs or simply ignored them.

"We think we'll just stay on here for a bit after the wedding," Marguerite said, poking ineffectually at her snowy white wig, which seemed to be slipping off center again. "After all, the lodge will be gone soon and this is our last chance to stay here."

Jane didn't know why they were telling her this or how she was expected to respond. They were free to stay until the bulldozers came up the driveway as far as Jane was concerned. She settled for a simple, "I see."

"We spent a lot of time here as girls, you see," Iva explained. "And we think we'd like some time to relive a few memories."

And search more thoroughly without interference, Jane thought.

"Take some nice walks in the fine weather . . ." Marguerite added.

Maybe they were just rehearsing their explanation to Jack, Jane speculated, and wondered if he was going to buy their story or pitch them out so *he* could have a last look around the place.

"That will be pleasant for you," Jane said mildly.

Uncle Joe had finished his beer and pretzels. He left the empty beer can on a side table and walked away.

"Well . . . good night," Iva said. She seemed dissatisfied with Jane's reaction to their plan.

"I think they expected you to argue with them," Shelley said when the elderly, bewigged pair had gone.

"I had that feeling, too. But why would I care? We'll be leaving after the wedding and the whole family can stay on if they want. I think they were practicing their story to tell Jack."

"It appears they haven't found what they're looking for yet," Shelley said.

"And they think they can really tear into the place when everyone else leaves," Jane agreed. "I wish them luck, I guess."

The bachelor party was breaking up. Jack and his friends were moving through the room to the front door and saying their good nights. Dwayne and his friends followed respectfully. Jane spotted one of the young men wiping his hand across his forehead in a "Whew! Thank God that's over!" gesture. Errol saw it, too, and laughed.

As the crowd was about to surge out the front door, Officer Smith came in. In full uniform. A silence fell on the whole group.

Smith smiled disarmingly and said, "Just checking on some loose ends, gentlemen." Mel emerged from the hallway to the small bedrooms and greeted Smith amiably. The two of them moved against the tide of departing guests, chatting casually. "Awfully late, isn't it?" Mel said.

"Just thought I'd stop by on my way home," Smith said, as though it were perfectly natural for him to be on his way home well after midnight.

But Jack Thatcher was furious. He glared at the two representatives of the law, then said to his coterie of friends, "Sightseers!" with a sarcastic laugh.

"I think it's time for us to go to bed," Shelley said.

"Absolutely," Jane said. She didn't want to be around when Jack's pals had left and the man had the leisure to let fly with his obvious outrage. "You don't need us for anything, do you?" she said to Mel in passing.

"Nope," he said.

Jane and Shelley fled to the relative safety of their adjoining rooms. "I wish there were locks on these doors," Shelley said, trying to shove a chair under the doorknob of her room. The chair was too short to be an effective wedge.

"You don't really think we're in danger of being murdered in our beds, do you?" Jane asked nervously.

"No, we don't know anything that's a threat to anyone, but I'd feel better if we were locked in."

"How do you know we're not a threat?" Jane asked. "We don't even know how Mrs. Crossthwait was a threat to somebody and we know a lot more about these people than she did."

"But we don't really know that, Jane. She could have had a long-buried history with someone in the family. Keep in mind about Marguerite and the wedding dress. Mrs. Crossthwait's story was true and Marguerite made much of not knowing her. She might have just forgotten because Mrs. Crossthwait was nothing but a minion, or she might have been in a full-fledged panic at running into her again after so long."

Shelley paused, thinking, then went on, "And for that matter, we aren't certain that she was killed because of something she knew. Maybe she just annoyed someone seriously unstable to the breaking point. Or reminded somebody of someone they loathed."

Jane went to her room and put on her nightgown. She was nervous about the final day of the wedding, which was looming only hours away. And she was sick to death of speculating about Mrs. Crossthwait's death. But it was like a hangnail on a grand and tragic scale. She couldn't make herself stop wondering and worrying about it and trying to pick at it. When she'd combed out her hair and brushed her teeth, she went into Shelley's room and perched on the end of the bed.

"We've been involved in murders before," she told Shelley, rather unnecessarily. "And we've figured them out. There were always suspects with good motives. But we've yet to come up with any motive for why someone would kill Mrs. Crossthwait. It's driving me slightly mad."

Shelley put down the paperback book she'd been pretending to read. "You're right. We've come up with dozens of rather stunningly stupid possibilities with absolutely nothing to back them up. You know what's troubling me the most?"

"What?"

"Whether there's some connection between the death of the seamstress and the trashing of Dwayne's room. I can't convince myself there's not a connection of some kind, but I simply cannot imagine what it could be. The first crime was so violent and final and the second was so trivial. It should have gone the other way, if you see what I mean."

"I think I do, but it was probably two different people with entirely different motives."

"I know it looks like that. But I have this strong gut feeling that they are related somehow," Shelley said. "I just can't formulate any reason why they should be."

Jane was quiet for a long moment. "The only thing the victims had in common, that we know of, is the wedding itself. Dwayne's role in it is obviously important, as the groom. Mrs. Crossthwait's was relatively minor. She was just making the dresses and they got finished even though she died. If there's a connection there, the crimes should have been the opposite way around."

"Right. If the point was to get rid of Dwayne and stop the wedding, he would have been the murder victim and the dresses might have been damaged or torn up as a little extra warning. Jane, it just doesn't make any kind of sense."

"It made sense to someone," Jane said. "Or to a couple of someones. Shelley, all I want is to get this wedding over with and go home. I'm considering making a sacred vow to never even attend another wedding the rest of my life."

Shelley grinned. "Be careful of those sacred vows. You've got three kids to marry off."

Jane put her head in her hands and groaned.

She was really trying desperately to get to sleep. And the harder she tried, the more wide awake she became. *Two o'clock,* Jane thought. *I have to get up in four and a half hours.* Then she worried that she would fall asleep so soundly she'd oversleep. She imagined the people coming to set up the tables, chairs, and linens and, without her guidance, getting everything all wrong. And what if Mr. Willis died in the night? Or Larkspur decided to suddenly move to Brazil instead of doing the flowers? Or the bridesmaids came down with malaria? Or Jack Thatcher decided the wedding was off? Finally, she fell into a light doze, dreaming of Larkspur in the jungle, giving medications to Kitty with a long, pointy flower. Kitty was lying on a sort of bier constructed of all her many pieces of luggage and swathed in yards of pink silk.

This dream was interrupted by footsteps in the hall. A man's footsteps, she thought. Should she get up and look? No. It was none of her business. She didn't care if some idiot chose to waste a good night's sleep. Then she heard Shelley stirring and the squeak of a floorboard.

Jane hopped out of bed. "Who went by?" she whispered into the darkness.

"I don't know."

There was a thin shaft of moonlight coming in the tiny window. Shelley was standing behind her door to the hall and holding her kerosene lantern over her head, ready to bash the skull of anyone who entered the room.

"Do you hear that?" Jane whispered. "A moaning sound."

"It's just the wind. This is a replay of last night," Shelley hissed.

"Look out the window. There's not a breath of wind."

"What should we do?" Shelley asked.

"Nothing?" Jane suggested.

"Somebody's moaning. Maybe they're hurt. Let's wake Mel up and make him check it out," Shelley said. "Where did you put him?"

"Two doors down. No, that's a bathroom door that's closed off. I think he's three doors down."

Shelley lit the kerosene lamp, very slowly and quietly opened the door, and stuck the lamp out into the hallway, in hopes of driving out anyone who might be lurking. She waited a moment, then peeked out. "Nobody in the hall," she said.

Jane clung to the back of Shelley's robe and they minced down the hall, the kerosene lamp casting eerie, jumpy shadows. Jane tapped lightly at Mel's door. There was no response. She tapped again, a little harder. Still no reaction. She took the lamp from Shelley and opened the door.

"There's nobody here," she said, peering inside the tiny room.

"You're sure?"

"Not unless he's curled up under the bed or hiding in the wardrobe."

"Check to make sure," Shelley said.

"Shelley! That's dumb!"

They heard the moaning again and clung to each other. Jane cocked her head, trying to figure out where the sound was coming from, but before she could determine anything, the door from the hallway to the main room creaked open. They were at the far end of the hall and could barely discern an amorphous gray shape, crouching in the doorway.

Shelley clutched Jane's arm so hard that Jane was sure she'd have permanent dents in her flesh.

"What the hell is that?" Shelley's whisper was so high-pitched that Jane half expected bats to appear to see who was talking to them.

"I hate to say it, but it looks to me like a ghost. A sort of dirty ghost," Jane said.

Shelley drew a deep breath, disengaged herself from her death grip on Jane, and suddenly strode forward, holding the lamp high above her head. "Get out of here!" she shouted at the apparition.

For good measure, she stamped her foot.

The figure whirled, clutched at its own chest, then yanked the door back open and fled.

"Wow!" Jane said. "Just like *Ghostbusters!*"

Two doors along the hallway were opened an inch or two. Jane was so disoriented she couldn't tell whose doors they were. And she was further distracted by the sound of a crash in the main room, and a shrill scream. Another bedroom door opened.

Jane and Shelley stared at each other for a long moment, silently debating whether to hide in their rooms or investigate. Naturally, they headed for the main room. As they approached the entrance, the door opened again. They drew back, thinking the ghost had changed its mind. But it was Mel who appeared in the doorway.

"Nothing to worry about," he said cheerfully. "Everybody just go back to bed."

Several doors closed quietly. He pointed to one that hadn't and it slammed shut.

"What on earth—" Jane began.

"Just some folks playing silly ass," he said. "You two are going to be comatose in the morning if you don't get some sleep."

"So are you," Jane snapped.

"Yes, but I have no responsibilities here. You do."

Jane was too tired to argue. She and Shelley found their rooms and Jane toppled into bed like a felled tree and was sound asleep before she could even wonder who the silly asses had been.

❖

Chapter 17

Jane was up at seven in the morning, not really awake, but vertical and dressed, which was the best she could manage. Although, as Shelley pointed out, she had her shirt on inside out. The struggle to get the sleeves turned right side out seemed almost insurmountable.

"Did I dream that ghostly figure last night?" Jane asked, fumbling at her buttons and wondering why her thumbs didn't seem to be working right.

"If so, it was a mutual dream."

"You were terrific," Jane said. "Just telling it to scat!"

"I was, wasn't I? What was Mel doing . . . roaming around in the middle of the night?"

"I don't know what anybody was doing. Are you ready for breakfast?"

Jane gathered her notebooks once again and the two of them headed for the kitchen, where Mr. Willis, chirpy as a chickadee, was just getting some freshly baked croissants out of the oven.

"Are we the first?" Jane asked.

He nodded as he set out a plate of the croissants as well as butter, cream cheese, and honey. Jane would normally have fallen on this feast like a starving barbarian, but today she was too preoccupied and only poured herself a cup of coffee. "The table and chair people are supposed to be here at nine. I wonder if I should call them."

"Jane, if they're coming at nine, they're already on their way. Don't fret. Eat. You need your strength."

Jane couldn't face food yet, and merely sat sipping her coffee and running down her mental list of what still remained to be done.

Iva and Marguerite came staggering into the kitchen, looking as tired as Jane felt. Iva had done something weird with her maroon wig, pulling some of the hair (if indeed it were hair, not polyester) down from the crown to form a sort of Veronica Lake sweep of bangs. It was extremely unattractive and as Iva sat down to eat, she kept fussing and pulling at it.

Jane was fascinated and kept staring at the older woman. When Mr. Willis asked Iva if she wanted straight coffee or decaf, Iva turned slightly to reply.

"Is there something wrong with your left eye?" Jane asked.

"No! What a rude personal remark!" Iva snapped.

"Sorry, but it looks like—"

"Mind your own business," Iva said, tugging at the bangs again.

The area around her left eye was heavily made up and it looked as if she'd used a good half a stick of blemish concealer above and below the eye. There was so much that it was caking. No wonder she was trying to hide it with her fake hair.

One of the local ladies who was helping Mr. Willis turned from where she was standing at the counter, rolling croissants, and said, "Oh, honey, you need to put some witch hazel on that. It'll take the swelling right down. And I'll make you up a nice little ice pack."

Iva flung her croissant on her plate and got up and walked out.

"Well! I never—" the helper exclaimed.

"What's wrong with your sister's eye?" Jane asked Marguerite.

"It's nothing. Nothing. She just ran into a chair."

"You're sure it wasn't a door?" Shelley asked wryly.

"No, she tripped getting into bed and fell against the chair," Marguerite said. "The back of the chair, the upright bit, hit her in the eye. It was just a freak accident. Nothing to worry about."

Marguerite sounded like a carefully rehearsed parrot.

"Lucky she didn't put her eye out," the helper said cheerfully, apparently believing the story. "I had a cousin got hit in the eye with the top end of a hoe. Never could see out of it again."

Nobody knew how to respond to this and a silence fell over the group.

"I think I better call the table and chair people," Jane said, having lost interest in Iva and still obsessing about her schedule.

As she left the room, she met Dwayne coming in. He looked as fresh and cheerful as new paint. "It's the big day," he said. Apparently he'd gone all "groomish" and forgotten about his room being trashed and holding Jane to blame.

"It is, indeed," Jane said.

"What was all that noise last night?" he asked. "People tromping up and down the hall at all hours."

"I don't really know," Jane said honestly. "I think there might have been a ghost at large."

He looked at her for a moment as if she'd lost her mind, then laughed. "Oh, I get it. A joke."

"Right," Jane said, trying to assemble a smile.

There was, naturally, no answer at the chair and table place. Jane told herself briskly that she shouldn't worry. It was too early for the secretary to be in the office and the truck was surely well on its way by now anyway. Still, she had visions of the truck sprawled on its side on a highway shoulder, tables and chairs scattered far and wide in the mud, perhaps a few curious cows browsing through the wreckage.

When she returned to the kitchen, the crowd had swelled. Marguerite had left, but Kitty, Eden, and Livvy had joined Shelley and Dwayne at the big table. Livvy looked wan and drained. She obviously hadn't gotten much sleep and was going to need some of Iva's concealer to cover the faint blue circles under her eyes. But as always, she was well put together in her rather starchy white blouse, black skirt, and stylish gray striped silk scarf as a belt. Jane suspected Livvy was probably even wearing panty hose.

Livvy smiled wanly at Jane. "Everything in order?" she asked politely.

"As far as I know," Jane said as confidently as she could manage. She hoped Livvy just wasn't a morning person and would perk up a whole lot as the day went on. Brides really shouldn't look like they needed to go back to bed—alone.

Dwayne was watching Livvy with concern, too. And Kitty looked upset as well, glancing back and forth between the two of them as she picked nervously at her breakfast. This annoyed Jane. Bridesmaids were supposed to rally around the bride, petting and encouraging them. Instead, Kitty looked like she herself were about to go to pieces. Jane thought of brisk, refreshing slaps that were sometimes delivered in movies to shape somebody up. Too bad it wasn't acceptable in real life.

Eden was another matter entirely. She'd come down in what might well have been her sleeping garments, an enormously oversized electric blue t-shirt with a Tweetie Bird logo on the front and baggy matching sweatpants. Her hair was uncombed and she looked tousled and sexy and was clearly the most cheerful person in the room. She was humming "Here Comes the Bride" as she tucked into her food and giving Livvy big, encouraging smiles.

Uncle Joe wandered through to pick up a free meal. He piled a plate high with croissants and a quarter of a stick of butter and then, to Jane's astonishment, he gave Livvy an affectionate little pat on the shoulder as he left. Livvy turned and smiled at him.

Jane couldn't believe Uncle Joe harbored a secret liking for anybody in the family. She wouldn't have thought he'd much more than barely noticed Livvy's existence, and yet the pat on the shoulder was clearly supportive. Could it be Uncle Joe who disapproved of Livvy's marriage to Dwayne? Might he have been the one who wrecked Dwayne's room in some hopeless attempt to make him feel unwelcome and possibly even drive him away?

And if that were true, was he also responsible for Mrs. Crossthwait's death? Or were she and Shelley wrong in thinking the two events were connected in any way? Uncle Joe had certainly been annoyed with Mrs. Crossthwait, but then he'd been annoyed with everyone. And Mel hadn't mentioned any sort of old or recent relationship between them after his gossip with the local law enforcement guys.

Still brooding over this, Jane finally got around to eating a croissant. That and another cup of hot, strong coffee would certainly get her brain cells to all wake up. She hoped.

The table and chair people arrived right on time and set about efficiently and quietly moving all the main room furniture back against the walls. They put the furniture in pleasant and attractive groupings, rather than letting it look like it was just shoved out of the way. Jane was impressed. She'd feared the room would end up looking like a warehouse.

The ivory folding chairs were set in tidy rows and really brightened the room. So did Larkspur's efforts. Since the bride and groom would be facing the audience, he arranged what he called a "frame" for them of flowers. Two very pretty potted willows to the side and a mass of hothouse tuberoses, white delphiniums, and tall pink cosmos in vases in front of the little trees. The wide stairway had a pot of pink tulips matching the bride's bouquet at the end of every other tread. Jane hadn't liked this idea when he proposed it because she was afraid the bride's skirt would brush against the pots and she'd arrive with dirt all over her. But the stairs were broad enough that Livvy would have to go well out of her way to kick the pots over. The flowers scented the musty room and looked lovely.

"For the first time, I feel this is actually going to work," Jane said as Shelley joined her in watching the transformation.

"I hate to say this, after all the jokes I've made, but it really looks grand," Shelley admitted. "Either Jack or Livvy must have sensed that this dismal old place could be made beautiful. Who'd have thought?"

Jane went to clean up, knowing the next few minutes would probably be her only free time. When she came out of her room in her lilac suit with the long flowered scarf, clean, curled hair, and a fast but pretty good makeup job, she ran into Mel in the hall. He was just coming out of his room.

"Wow! You look great!" he said.

"Why, thank you," she said, doing a little pirouette, hoping to elicit further compliments.

What she got was a kiss that made a mess of her lipstick and threatened her hairdo. She pulled away, grinning. "Now I'm going to have to start over."

"Need some help?"

"No, thanks," Jane said with a laugh. Then, more seriously, she asked, "What did John Smith think of the seam binding Shelley and I found in the attic?"

"Just what you thought. That it was probably stretched across the stairs and then removed. It doesn't give him any leads on who the perp was, but it'll come in handy when he knows that and it goes to court. It indicates planning, rather than sudden passion."

" 'Sudden passion' doesn't seem a phrase that has much to do with Mrs. Crossthwait. So who was the ghost last night?"

"Uncle Joe. In a gray blanket. He was being the ghost of a monk for the benefit of his half-sisters."

"Benefit?"

"His benefit, actually. They'd apparently been talking about staying on for a while. He remembered them as girls, getting themselves all in a twit over ghosts of monks, and thought it might scare them off."

"He told you this?"

"Not very willingly. And he was pissed as hell that it was you and Shelley who came out of your rooms instead of them. Silly old man."

"Have you run into Iva this morning?" Jane asked.

"With the shiner?"

"Right. What happened to her?"

"That was later. She was prowling around doing God knows what and saw a light in the pantry. She'd gotten on her knees to try to peer through the keyhole. Joe was in there, heard scuffling, and opened the door. Got her in the eye with the doorknob. They both confirmed that story."

"Have you been up all night long trailing around after them?" Jane asked.

"Most of the night."

"Why? Why not let them just barge around running into each other?"

Mel put his arm around her shoulders and said, "Because one of them could very well be a killer and you don't have a lock on your door."

"You stayed up all night to protect me? Oh, Mel—"

"Don't go sappy and get any ideas about my making a habit of it," he said. "We're all out of here this evening. And the next time I miss another night's sleep for your sake, it's going to be for much more enjoyable reasons."

Chapter 18

Luncheon was a hasty, eat-on-the-run affair, complicated by the fact that several of the out-of-town guests, bored senseless at their cheap little motel which didn't even have cable television, as they kept saying to each other with wonder, came early and got underfoot. The two musicians, a married couple from Novelties, whom Jane had nearly forgotten about, turned up with a flute and violin. They were attired in black and looked like they'd come for a funeral.

Jane went down the hallway to the little rooms to check that everyone was getting along all right. Everybody was trying to get cleaned up at once and since all were on the same water supply along the hallway, there were occasional yelps and shouts as toilets were flushed in some rooms at the same time showers were going on in others.

In spite of everything bad that had happened, Jane sensed a genuine air of festivity now. Layla and Eden kept running up and down the hall in their bathrobes like schoolgirls in a dorm, borrowing toothpaste, hair spray, and makeup. Kitty in particular seemed obsessed with looking as good as possible. "I think this hem is uneven," she wailed at Jane.

"Nobody will notice and it's too late to fix it," Jane said mildly, even though Kitty was nearly in tears. She had lost patience with Kitty. It was the bride who was supposed to be hysterical, not the bridesmaids.

Mel popped out of his room asking if he could help her with anything.

"No, thanks. I'm just looking for brushfires to put out. And not, thank God, finding any yet."

Jane went through the main room. Early guests sat in the chairs and sofas around the sides of the room, keeping the wedding chairs inviolate. Jane went upstairs to the master bedroom to see if she could help Livvy. "Is there anything you need before you get dressed? Hairpins? Perfume?" Jane asked.

Livvy was sitting at the window, gazing out as if bored. "What? Oh, no. But thanks anyway."

"Are you okay, Livvy?"

The young woman smiled weakly. "I'm fine. Just fine. I'll just need help getting into the dress when it's time."

"Have you had lunch?"

"I think so. Yes, yes. A sandwich. I've heard some cars arriving. Should I be greeting guests?"

Jane laughed. "No, it's like a play, Livvy. The lead actress isn't seen until the curtain goes up. She doesn't hang around in the lobby."

Livvy's smile was genuine this time.

She's just nervous, Jane told herself, going back down

the wide steps Livvy would descend in an hour. Brides were supposed to be nervous. Livvy was about to commit herself in the most important ceremony in her life. Baptisms, recitals, even hard-won graduations were nothing compared to wedding ceremonies for making everyone nervous. Marriages often failed later. Jane's own marriage had failed without her even realizing it until it was too late. But going into marriage, saying vows, and observing the ancient rites still had the power to seem a "forever" decision.

For the first time in a long, long while, Jane found herself thinking about her own wedding, a few weeks short of twenty years ago now. Her mother had wept. Jane thought it was from happiness, but it might not have been. Her father had treated her like a porcelain doll and told her that she'd always be his daughter, no matter whose wife or mother she became. Her sister Marty had worn a red dress she knew Jane hated. Typical of Marty. Her mother-in-law Thelma had worn a gray dress, but obviously longed to wear black. It had been an even smaller wedding than Livvy's because Steve's family lived in Chicago and Jane's only family were her parents, sister, grandmother, and honorary uncle Jim. And it had been held in the Jeffry family's church without all the elaborate flowers and catering. But Jane still remembered every moment of it with fondness. She'd even liked Marty and Thelma that day.

She'd married Steve Jeffry because he was handsome, ambitious, polite, and because he asked her at the exact right moment of her life. She'd been too young and stupid, really, to make such an important decision, but after having grown up all over the world—beloved by her parents, but forever homeless, rootless—she was desperately longing to be a wife. To have a husband, a home, and have lots of plump, pretty babies who grew up in a neighborhood with lifelong friends and schoolmates, not a gigantic circle of slight acquaintances like she'd had.

Livvy's situation was quite different. She was a much older bride, for starters. She'd sensibly dedicated herself to preparing for a career and been a successful businesswoman for a number of years. She'd have her babies, too, with any luck, but because it was demanded of her. Jane wasn't sure that would make for a better marriage.

"You look very thoughtful," Shelley said, startling her.

Jane had sat down on the bottom step of the staircase. Shelley joined her.

"I was thinking about weddings," Jane said. "Livvy's and my own."

"I don't dare think about mine," Shelley said. "My mother organized it as if it were the second D Day invasion. Tried to make the bridesmaids all look like clones of me. Even expected my cousin Zoe to dye her hair."

"No!"

Shelley shook her head and laughed. "No, I made it up to get you out of your funk. I think this is going to go well. Have you seen Dwayne?"

"Not since breakfast."

"He's already in his tux and I must admit he looks very spiffy and groomish."

"And the girls? Are they ready?"

"Yes. Kitty spilled some soda on the sleeve of her jacket and went to pieces. I gave her some home truths about just who was the center of attention here and was meant to be noticed, and who wasn't, and left Layla cleaning her up."

"Why's she so het up?"

"I think this is the only wedding she's ever been in," Shelley said. "And I suspect she fears it will be the last. She's really not very attractive and hasn't the personality to overcome that drawback. You and I know a number of women who aren't very good-looking, but knock the socks off every man they meet by sheer charm. Kitty isn't one of them."

They'd been more or less hidden behind the flowers and the small lectern the minister would be standing at and now Jane heard someone saying her name. She sighed and stood up. "I'm right here, Mr. Thatcher."

He left the people he'd been talking to and approached her. "I've been looking everywhere for you. Is Livvy ready?"

"She'll be ready in time. I'm just getting the girls to help her dress."

Layla and Eden were in high spirits and even Kitty seemed to have pulled herself together. "People are arriving. I want you out of sight so you can make a grand entrance," Jane said. "Let's go to Livvy's room and all help her get her gown and veil on."

They hurried through the main room and upstairs. Jane took a seat by the door while the younger women fussed with Livvy's petticoats, a fancy garter, and the dress. As Eden started working on the long row of tiny buttons up the back, there was a light tap on the door. Mr. Willis had brought up an iced silver bucket with a bottle of champagne and a tray of elegant glasses.

"My gift to the bride and bridesmaids," he said.

They all thanked him effusively. "No more than a sip or we'll all be too drunk to get down the stairs without tripping," Eden said with a laugh. Then, realizing this might have been tactless considering how Mrs. Crossthwait had met her end, she started apologizing.

Jane took charge and cut her off. "There's no time for any of you to get tipsy," she said. "It's only ten minutes until showtime. Livvy, you look spectacular. And the rest of you are beautiful." She opened the door and said, "Whispering only now."

There was a short stretch of wall between Livvy's room and the head of the stairs where they could line up without being seen from the room below. "Layla first, then Eden, then Kitty, remember. Here comes your father, Livvy."

The husband and wife musicians were seated far enough back from the top of the stairs to be out of the way, but close enough for their music to drift down the stairway. Jane got the bridesmaids, Livvy, and her father lined up, took a deep breath, and nodded to the couple.

They stood up and began to play the flute and violin quietly. As the volume of chat and shuffling about in the room below diminished, the music got louder. After a moment, Jane peeked around the corner. The guests were in place. Marguerite and Iva sat to one side of the front row of chairs, Iva in a floor-length silvery dress and Marguerite in a matching style but in maroon. They should have traded either wigs or dresses, Jane thought. Mrs. Hessling was sitting on the other side of the aisle in dreadfully violent turquoise polyester with quite a large matching hat and purse. She was fidgeting with the purse, obviously trying to figure out whether she should hang onto it or set it on the floor. Uncle Joe, wearing the fairly decent clothes he'd worn to the rehearsal dinner, was standing against a wall at the back of the room, looking around at the other guests with a scowl. As Jane watched, Dwayne, Errol, and the minister came out of the side room where Shelley had been holding them until the right moment.

"Okay," Jane whispered as she turned to face the upstairs contingent. "Layla, you first. Try to stay centered on the staircase."

Layla, lovely in her pink slip dress with the fringed scarf draped skillfully over one shapely shoulder, stepped out, head held high, and started slowly and gracefully down the stairs.

Jane watched for a moment, counting to ten, and turned to Eden. "You're next."

Livvy was whispering furiously to her father. "I can't do it, Daddy. I know you're disappointed, but—"

"Livvy, get a grip on yourself," he said quietly, but very sharply.

"No. I don't want to marry Dwayne. I don't want to marry anyone."

Jane nearly fainted. She'd already launched the first bridesmaid and it was time to fire up the next one and the bride had changed her mind!

There hadn't been *anything* in the wedding planning books about this!

Eden had turned to them as well. "Good for you, Livvy. Good for you!"

"Butt out, Eden," Jack Thatcher said. "You've always been a troublemaker."

"Daddy—"

"Livvy, it's too late. The wedding has started."

The musicians, fascinated and appalled by the argument, missed a few notes. Jane glared at them and they obediently looked away and went back to playing properly.

"But Daddy—"

"No, Livvy. I'm not going to let you humiliate all of the family this way."

Kitty made a funny gasping noise. Her face was awash in tears. Jane lunged into Livvy's room and grabbed a box of tissues, handing a wad of them to Kitty.

Eden took Jane's arm. "I'm going down now. The guests are starting to get alarmed and Jack will win anyway."

She stepped out onto the stairway and started down the steps. Jane pulled on Kitty's sleeve, took another handful of tissues and quickly blotted her face, and said, "If you don't smile as you go down those steps, I'll hunt you down later and slap you senseless. Do you understand me?"

Kitty nodded and composed her face into a rather horrible grimace.

Jane didn't even have to watch Kitty's descent to know how awkward it was. She could hear the clunk of her feet over the music which was relentlessly going on. She turned to Livvy and Jack.

The hissing match was over. Livvy had one hand resting lightly on her father's arm and was holding her tulip bouquet in the other hand. Her face was as cold, white, and composed as marble. Jane waited, staring at them with horrified fascination, and when the sound of Kitty's heavy steps stopped, she touched Livvy's arm. It was clammy.

"Are you sure?" Jane asked.

Before Jack could say anything, Livvy nodded and father and daughter stepped forward.

Jane couldn't bear to even watch them descend the staircase. It was too much like watching someone go to the gallows. She went back to Livvy's room and collapsed in the chair by the window.

"Poor, poor Livvy," she whispered.

The musicians reached the end of their piece and fell silent.

Chapter 19

If Livvy refused to say her vows or ran screaming out of the lodge when the minister said, "Do you, Livvy . . ." there would be nothing Jane could do. Nor did she want to be seen peeking around the wall again, so she just sat there staring out the window, as clever and nimble as an amoeba, until the musicians began to play again.

That meant it was over. For better or worse. If Jane's plans had been followed, Livvy and Dwayne had kissed to seal the bargain, then come around their flower "frame" and exited the lodge down the little center aisle between the chairs. In a moment, they'd be outside in the lovely April sunshine, being congratulated as the guests poured out behind them to deliver hugs, kisses, and good wishes.

Livvy was going to need lots of good wishes.

Jane bestirred herself. There was a lot to do now and very little time. As she came down the stairs, she saw that the table people were already scurrying around like a school of very organized fish to fold up the chairs and stack them in preparation for putting up the long buffet table.

Larkspur was standing by, practically dancing with impatience and holding a big flower arrangement. At least Jane assumed it was Larkspur. All she could see were his legs behind the vase, flowers, and foliage.

Likewise, Mr. Willis was hovering at the kitchen door with an enormous silver chafing dish and his local assistant was weighed down with a stack of dinner plates.

Shelley was doing her best to dislodge the few guests who hadn't yet moved outside. "I'm tempted to jerk their chairs out from under them," she said as she passed Jane. "Ladies, would you like to come outside now?" she cooed sweetly to a pair of the trophy wives who were comparing their jewelry.

As soon as the last of them were driven outdoors, chaos broke out.

The long tables were slammed into place in the center of the room, tablecloths snapped and billowed and before they were even all in place, Mr. Willis and Larkspur were fighting for space on the long white expanse. Mr. Willis thought the beef Stroganoff should have pride of place in the very center of the table with appetizers and salads on one side and bread and desserts on the other. Larkspur felt strongly, and was not loath to express the view as if it were gospel, that the enormous vase of tulips, ferns, and agapanthus must be the center highlight with smaller arrangements in the spots Mr. Willis had marked out for the plates, silverware, and napkins at the far end.

"Centerpiece flowers in the center," Jane snapped. "Small arrangements between the plates and appetizers and another between the bread and desserts and stop squabbling! Larkspur, the drinks table is almost ready. You work on that and then fit things around what Mr. Willis sets out."

"No flowers near the glasses," Mr. Willis shrieked. "They'll drop petals and bugs in the glassware."

"My flowers do *not* have bugs!"

"Flowers in the middle, glasses around them. Flower petals in champagne look pretty," Jane declared.

"You're getting this bossy stuff down," Shelley said from behind her. "What was the big delay between Layla's entrance and Eden's? People were beginning to mutter among themselves."

"Livvy was pleading with her father to cancel the wedding," Jane said with a heavy sigh.

"No!" Shelley exclaimed. "She wanted to bolt at the very last second?"

"Yes, it was ghastly. Eden was encouraging her, Kitty was weeping, the musicians were eavesdropping, I was considering pretending to faint, and in the end, Jack prevailed."

"Of course he did."

"And Livvy's stuck with Dwayne," Jane said grimly.

Shelley thought for a minute and said, "Jane, maybe it was just momentary panic on Livvy's part. A burst of quick hysteria that she really didn't mean. If she really and truly didn't want to marry him, surely she'd have brought it to a halt a lot sooner. When you got married didn't you have just a second when you thought, 'What am I *doing!*' "

"No, I thought I knew exactly what I was doing. I was wrong, of course, but I didn't have a second's doubt."

Shelley patted Jane's arm. "Well, I hate to be hard-hearted, but it's done now and it's not your problem. Livvy had a decision to make and she made it. Period. Now she's

Mrs. Dwayne Hessling, whether she likes it or not. You're neither her mother nor her best friend and you couldn't have interfered."

"But the sad thing is, she doesn't have a mother or a best friend," Jane said. "And she needed both."

The food was in place and smelled divine. The flowers were on the serving tables and Larkspur had placed small arrangements on some of the end tables as well. The furniture people had completed their work and slipped out a side door. They'd come back tomorrow at their leisure and Uncle Joe would let them in to pick up all the rental furniture and linens. The wedding cake, all four tiers of it, sat in solitary splendor in the side room, among the gifts on display.

Jane took one last look around. Perfection. And best of all, this was the last stage of the process. Everybody would be fed and the bride and groom would be seen off to their honeymoon and Jane could go home, cash the check for the last part of her fee, and forget she'd ever been insane enough to get involved in a stranger's wedding. She wondered if she could persuade her children to elope when the time came. A nice monetary bribe ought to do it.

Finally at ease, she went to the front door and opened it. The photographer was taking one last picture of the entire wedding party assembled on a slight slope so they fanned up the hill behind Livvy and Dwayne. Livvy was either happy now or giving a decent impression of looking as if she were. Dwayne was beaming. Some kind soul had relieved Mrs. Hessling of her huge, horrible handbag.

Jane had the fleeting thought that maybe she should

get a copy of this picture and put it in Mrs. Crossthwait's scrapbook as the old woman would have liked. But who was left to care what was in the book? It would probably end up in a garage sale and some antiques dealer would buy it to use the old pictures with old frames he was trying to sell.

The guests were getting hungry and were milling closer to the door. As the last picture was taken, Jane called out, "Will the bride and groom lead everyone back into the lodge?"

There were a few grumbles from those closest to the door, who were the hungriest, but they turned into exclamations of pleased surprise as the crowd flowed back into the lodge and discovered the miraculous transformation of the room.

As soon as most of the guests had gone along the food line, Jane checked with Mr. Willis that everything in the kitchen was in order. He assured her that it was and trays of second helpings of anything they might run out of were warming or cooling, as appropriate. Jane left the kitchen, then came to a stop. She'd been in the mode of thinking of all the things she must do and which would come next for days now, and suddenly, there was nothing for her to do.

Nothing!

She smiled blissfully and sank into the nearest chair and very nearly fell asleep.

When everybody was through eating, she'd have to round them up and head them to the side room where the magnificent cake awaited unveiling. There would be a few toasts, the photographer would take pictures of the ceremonial cake cutting, everybody would have a nibble, and then it would be time for the guests to start drifting away.

These happy thoughts were suddenly and violently interrupted by what Jane first thought to be a siren, but was a piercing scream that went on and on and on. There was a horrified silence in the main room. Jane leaped to her feet and ran to the closed door of the side room, colliding with Shelley and Mel as she reached it.

Mel opened the door just wide enough for the three of them to slip in, then slammed it behind them.

Kitty was standing with her back to them in the center of the room, shrieking. Dwayne was sprawled at her feet, his eyes closed, a huge red stain spread across his white shirt. Mel stepped forward and took her arm. She turned to him with a knife in her hand. She stopped screaming and started whimpering. He pinched the blade of the knife between two fingers and she released it, looking down at it with horror. Mel bent to put down the knife and examine Dwayne. "Shelley, call 911," he said calmly.

Kitty drifted backwards, her eyes still on Dwayne, and backed into Jane.

Livvy and Jack had pushed through the crowd and entered the room. Jack stood with his back to the door, keeping anyone else from entering. Livvy had one hand over her mouth and was clutching her father's sleeve with the other.

Kitty turned to Jane. Hiccupping and crying, she said, "Someone s-said the cake was beautiful. I—I wanted to look before it was cut. I c-came in. Dwayne was there. On the f-floor. I thought he'd f-fainted."

"Calm down, Kitty," Jane said.

"Then I l-looked. There was a knife in his ch-chest."

Her voice had risen to a shriek again. "I pulled it out. I thought it would s-save him. B-but there was all that blood."

"You shouldn't have touched it," Jane said, averting her eyes from Dwayne.

"I know. I know. But I thought—" She looked over Jane's shoulder.

"Livvy, why did you have to do this?" Kitty asked.

Livvy made a noise like a mouse caught in a trap. A little squeak. Then said, "Me? Me! You think I stabbed my husband?"

"You could have divorced him," Kitty said, sobbing. "You could have had the marriage annulled. You didn't have to kill him."

Livvy's eyes rolled back and she slipped to the floor in a heap.

Mel sent Jane to guard the front door and make sure no one left.

"Is he dead?" she whispered.

"Very."

The guests were babbling hysterically. Several grabbed at Jane as she passed through the crowd around the door.

"What's happened?" "Who was screaming?" they asked.

"There's been an accident," she said loudly, her voice shaking. "Keep the doorway clear. Don't anybody leave." She had to pluck several hands off her sleeve to get away.

She could already hear sirens when she reached the door. Iva Thatcher had followed Jane and said, in a frail, trembling voice, "It's not Livvy, is it?"

Jane gave Iva a quick hug. "No, no. It's not Livvy. It's Dwayne. I'm afraid he's dead."

"Dead! How?"

Jane didn't want Iva starting a riot of rumor. "I don't know," Jane lied.

Two police cars and an ambulance pulled up as well as a beat-to-hell green Plymouth. A very short, tough-looking elderly man got out of the car. Jane guessed it was Gus Ambler, the old sheriff Mel had gotten the background on the Thatchers from.

"Where is the victim?" John Smith asked.

Jane pointed the way and stood aside as he and the ambulance attendants rushed past. The old man was last and puffing with the effort to hurry.

"I'm with the police," he said gruffly.

"I thought so," Jane said, letting him pass. She couldn't have stopped his headlong rhinoceros progress if she'd tried.

She closed the door and leaned back against it with her eyes closed. If she'd had her car keys in her possession at that moment, she might well have grabbed Shelley and staggered to her rusty, familiar station wagon and driven away.

Chapter 20

It was the longest afternoon and evening of Jane's life.

The Thatcher family and everybody else who had been known to be in the lodge when Mrs. Crossthwait died had been told in no uncertain terms that they had to stay until the next day. It went far beyond mere coincidence that two murders should occur within the same group of people without there being a connection. Jane and Shelley took their turns at calling home and explaining that they would be delayed another day. Jane didn't elaborate to her mother-in-law why this was. She just let her think it was to finish off all the loose ends.

She overheard Layla on the phone a few minutes later, sobbing to her husband that she wanted to come home to him and the babies. Shortly after Layla's call, she spotted Eden on the phone, talking very quietly and intensely, funneling her words into the mouthpiece with her hand so as to not be overheard.

Everyone present had to be questioned. The guests were all upset and some of them wasted a lot of time being indignant and rude out of sheer fright and the desire to get away. The off-duty police officers were called in and the county sheriff's office sent a scene-of-the-crime unit.

Mrs. Hessling was too grief-stricken to even speak coherently and Errol begged the police to let her go back to the motel. The coroner, who was also the local doctor, had shown up and supported the idea, even supplying Errol with a mild sedative to give her.

Surprisingly, Iva got involved. "You must stay with your brother's . . . body," she told Errol. "It isn't decent to leave him with strangers. I'll take your mother back and keep an eye on her while my sister watches over Livvy."

Mr. Willis and Larkspur both attempted to escape on the grounds that they had business scheduled for the next day, but were told it was too bad and they better get in touch with their assistants or partners and instruct them to take over. They did so with very bad grace.

The guests were all given paper and pencils and asked to write down everything they'd seen and heard, no matter how trivial, from the moment the photographer took the group picture until Kitty had started screaming.

Most of them had only the vaguest recollection of what they'd noticed. A few admitted they'd had too much champagne to remember much. Some wrote virtual tomes of "he said and then I said." Each had to give his or her written report to one of the off-duty officers, who read them, asked additional questions about times and locations, and made a red check mark at the top of the first page. This was what Jane, feeling very much like a prison guard, had to collect before people were allowed to leave in twos and threes.

Between departures, she skimmed through the reports

and decided it was going to take a much better mind than hers to fit the various stories together and deduce anything coherent from them. It seemed that Kitty wasn't the only one who had heard how spectacular the wedding cake was and sneaked into the side room to take a look at it in its uncut glory. Several observers claimed they'd seen Layla go in the room. Others described someone who was obviously Eden going through the door.

One trophy wife, whose handwriting suggested she was way beyond mere tipsiness, claimed she'd seen Jack Thatcher go in the room in a most "furtive" manner, looking about to make sure no one saw him. But a great many of the other reports mentioned having spoken to Jack in the main room at one time or another. Jane wondered when he could have found time to skulk into the side room when he was so busy being the gracious host. She also wondered if the woman had a husband in a position to benefit financially if Jack Thatcher were arrested for murder.

Two people said they'd seen Layla go up the stairs to the second floor, another claimed to have seen Eden come down the stairs. Although their looks and dresses were really quite different, apparently the bridesmaids in their pink dresses were indistinguishable to the casual observer. One of the groomsmen claimed he'd been sitting on the second step talking to a pretty girl whose name he couldn't remember and that nobody went up or down the stairs.

Two people said they'd seen a seedy-looking groundskeeper-type hanging around the doorway, but none of them came right out and said they'd seen him go into the room. Jane assumed this was Uncle Joe.

Only one man had paid the least attention to time. He, a clock freak, asked for extra paper and outlined to the minute who he'd talked to, what they said, what they were wearing, but admitted he had his back to the side room the whole time and couldn't have seen anyone coming or going.

Oddly enough, no one, so far, had mentioned having seen Dwayne himself go into the side room. And he obviously had. There was a side door to the room, but it was stuck firmly shut, as Jane had discovered during the bridal shower when she tried to open it to get a little fresh air in. But if nobody noticed Dwayne enter, it might well be that nobody noticed the killer going in either.

There was eventually only a handful of disgruntled guests remaining and their accounts were being read and questioned. Jack was pacing the main room furiously, muttering about the general incompetence of the police. Marguerite had helped Livvy remove her wedding gown and the bride was now in pressed, creased jeans and a plaid shirt. She should have been in her pale blue "going away" suit long since.

Livvy was sitting on a sofa, looking stunned. Errol was trying to get her to eat something. As Jane watched, Livvy waved away a plate of food and suddenly burst into tears. Errol put the plate down, sat next to her, and patted her shoulder rather awkwardly and ineffectually.

Mr. Willis was clearing away the food and Larkspur was dismantling the floral arrangements. Jane guessed that they felt, as she did, that the wedding paraphernalia was now in very bad taste, considering that the groom was dead. Perhaps at the hand of the bride, if Kitty's accusation was to be believed. But could Livvy, the centerpiece of the wedding, have sneaked away without being noticed?

Wouldn't that big white dress have been a sort of beacon? And wouldn't it have shown blood?

The last guests handed in their reports and left. And a few minutes later a sheet-covered gurney took Dwayne away. Jane noticed that Errol made a point of standing in front of Livvy, blocking her view, as this terrible departure took place. He was a very considerate young man.

Jane went to the side room, tapped on the door, and handed the reports over to Mel. "I've read a bunch of them. Practically nobody agrees on anything."

Mel wasn't surprised. "We do a public service class from time to time to show people how the law enforcement agencies work," he said. "In one of the sessions, the attendees are warned that a fake argument will take place during the hour and they are to observe closely. Later a man and woman enter the room, squabbling, and he drags her out the other door. When the attendees write up their impressions, they're almost always way, way wrong. Wrong color hair, heights, weights, clothing. And they've been *told* it was going to happen and to observe closely."

"Then what's the point of the reports here?" Jane asked.

"First, to get an impression of the people writing them . . ."

"That certainly works."

"And sometimes they get things right, if you're patient enough to piece them all together."

"Good luck," Jane told him.

Shelley had been helping clear the tables, picking up glasses, dishes, ashtrays, and silverware and taking them to the kitchen. Now she joined Jane.

"We should pack up the gifts," she said.

"The police are using the room to interview people," Jane said.

"Yes, I know that, Jane. That's why I made the suggestion."

"You think they'd let us eavesdrop?" Jane asked.

"Maybe. If we were very quiet and very busy and didn't appear to be listening."

"There's nothing to lose by trying," Jane said.

They went to the door with armloads of boxes. Jane banged on the door with her elbow. "May we leave these in here?" she asked when Mel opened the door.

He grinned. "Just leave them?"

"Well, pack a few things, maybe," Jane said with a straight face.

Jane could see Kitty sitting on one of the rental chairs, twisting a handkerchief in her hands as John Smith sat across from her, asking questions.

"I told you already. Over and over," Kitty was saying in a weak, tear-ravaged voice. "You ought to be talking to Livvy instead of me. I only came in here to look at the cake. I saw Dwayne lying on the floor. I thought he'd had too much to drink and passed out or something and went to him. Then I saw the knife and I pulled it out. I wasn't thinking. I guess something told me I could make it better that way. It was stupid, I know . . ."

"We'll move to another room pretty soon, Jane. Just leave the boxes by the door," Mel said.

"Well, nothing ventured, nothing gained," Shelley said with a shrug.

"Don't you hate it when trite things are true?" Jane commented, unloading her boxes onto the floor.

The phone rang and Jane, who was closest to it, picked it up reluctantly. "Thatcher Lodge," she said.

A harried-sounding voice came over the line.

"Yes, she's here," Jane said, "but she's not able to come to the phone right now. May I take a message?" Jane listened for a moment, perplexed, then started making frantic "pencil and paper" motions at Shelley.

"I'm sorry. I'm not authorized to give that information without permission. Let me call you back in a moment."

She scribbled a woman's name, a newspaper name, and a telephone number, and said, "I'll get back to you as soon as I can."

"A reporter?" Shelley sneered.

"Not exactly," Jane said, staring at the paper. "The society editor of a Chicago paper. Wanting to confirm a wedding announcement."

"I thought you'd already taken care of that," Shelley said.

"I have. It's to appear this Sunday in a different paper. And with a different bride."

"What on earth are you talking about?"

"The editor wanted to confirm the details and spelling of the names of the bride and groom: Katherine Louise Wilson and Dwayne Hessling."

"What? Who's this Katherine person?"

"Kitty."

"Oh, Jane, they just mixed up the bridesmaid with the bride."

Jane shook her head. "No, Shelley. I was in charge of the announcements and I never turned one in to this paper. Somebody *else* mixed up who was the bridesmaid and who was the bride at this wedding."

❖

Chapter 21

Jane knocked on the door of the side room again. This time Mel looked distinctly cranky. "What now?" he asked, stepping through the doorway and closing the door.

"I've learned something you really should know."

He didn't look heavenward, but it was a near thing. "Okay, let me have it," he said.

But when Jane was through explaining about the phone call, he lost his impatience. "You're certain you didn't call this in wrong?"

"It's just a little local suburban paper. Almost a shopper. I had no reason to contact them." She gave him the name of the newspaper. "Nobody there would be interested."

"Except that it's where Kitty lives," Mel said.

"No!" Jane exclaimed. "I guess I didn't pay much attention to her address. Come to think of it, I mailed her sample fabric to a post office box. I think."

"Now, Jane, think hard. You're one hundred percent sure this isn't just a mistake of yours? You looked up a newspaper number and maybe accidentally dialed the one before or the one after?"

"I didn't dial anyone. I sent the engagement photo and typed up the information to mail. I couldn't have accidentally addressed it to a paper I had no intention of notifying."

"Okay, wait here."

A few moments later, he was back. "I told Smith about the call. He wants you to come in the room in about five minutes and convey the phone message to Kitty. No questions. No elaboration. Just tell her what the person on the phone said."

Shelley grabbed Jane's arm and said, "You're not going in there without me."

They waited the required five minutes. Jane had made a copy of the information she'd written down. She knocked on the door and they entered without waiting for permission. Jane handed Kitty the copy. "This person called for you, Kitty."

Kitty only glanced at the note. "Who is this?"

"The society editor of your local newspaper. She wanted to be sure she had your name and Dwayne's spelling right in your wedding announcement."

Kitty looked at her blankly. "I don't understand."

"Someone called in and gave her the wording for an announcement that you and Dwayne had gotten married this weekend."

"You've made some mistake. Or they did when you called."

"I never contacted them," Jane said.

"Who did?" Kitty asked.

At this point, John Smith interrupted. "You know, I

wouldn't be surprised if they record those calls, just to be able to review the information when they write it up. Maybe I should ask for a dupe . . ."

Kitty looked stricken.

"Do you have something else to tell us?" Smith asked calmly.

Kitty slumped and put her hands to her face, sobbing. Nobody spoke. They waited impatiently for her to pull herself together. Finally she raised her head and said, shakily, "Okay. Okay. I'll tell you the truth. Dwayne and I were in love. We were going to get married. But neither of us had much money and we wanted a house and children and—well, we came up with a plan."

"When?" Smith asked.

"A year ago. I introduced him to Livvy. He pretended to be crazy about her. See, I'd overheard her father harping on her about how it was time to get married and give him grandchildren. We thought—Dwayne and I—that if he managed to get engaged to her, her father would pay him off to get lost. Jack Thatcher is such a damned snob. And Jack did try to get rid of Dwayne, but wouldn't pay enough."

Jane and Shelley exchanged astonished looks, but kept quiet.

"Dwayne said when it came closer to the wedding, he knew Thatcher would get desperate enough to up the ante."

"And he didn't?" Smith asked calmly.

"No, not enough. So Dwayne and I talked it over last night and decided he'd better go through with the wedding, and then he could divorce her and get a big settlement out of the family."

"There wasn't a prenuptial agreement?" Gus Ambler snapped. Jane hadn't even noticed him sitting in the far corner of the room until he spoke.

Kitty shook her head. "No, Jack wanted one, but Dwayne refused to sign it. He knew they'd cut him off with nothing if he signed anything. That's why he thought up to the very end that Jack would put a stop to the wedding. Then we were going to take the money and get married right away. We'd had our blood tests and the marriage license and everything."

She paused. They were all silent in the face of this confession.

"I know it wasn't nice," Kitty said, sniffling again. "But we were so desperately in love and so poor. And Livvy didn't really care anything about him. Jane, you heard her. Just before she went down the stairs, she tried to back out of the wedding and her father wouldn't let her. She didn't love him at all and he didn't care anything about her. He was in love with me. It was the only way we could get married and have a house and children. I know you all must think we were awful, but it was the only thing we could do. We had to."

She looked around for sympathy or understanding and found nothing but perfectly blank expressions.

"I didn't think Livvy would care," Kitty went on. "She didn't want to marry him. You know that, Jane. You heard her say so. Eden heard it, so did the musicians, I imagine. But Dwayne must have told her sometime during the reception dinner that he wanted a divorce right away and was leaving with me. All that prissy repression must have burst the dam. She was furious at being made a fool of and she killed him. I'm not sure she even meant to, really.

I can understand. She was so shocked, so embarrassed, and there was that knife we used to cut the ribbons on the presents and . . ."

She dissolved in tears again. "And now neither of us can have him. I don't know how I'll live without him. I'd rather she'd have killed me."

If she expected sympathy, she was disappointed. There was an almost palpable air of disgust in the room.

John Smith looked at Jane. "Would you mind finding Mr. Thatcher and asking him to come in here?"

Jane did as she was asked. Jack Thatcher was still in the main room. "Mr. Thatcher, the police would like to speak to you."

"Well, it's about time!" he snarled.

She followed him back to the side room. He started complaining the moment he passed through the doorway, but John Smith cut him off. "Mr. Thatcher, did your daughter and Dwayne Hessling have a prenuptial agreement?"

"What? What difference does that make? Of course they did."

"Could I see it?"

"Good God, man! I'm not carrying the damned thing around with me! It's in the safe deposit box at my bank."

"No!" Kitty exclaimed. "He's lying. Dwayne told me he'd absolutely refused to sign anything."

Thatcher turned to her, looking as if he couldn't quite remember who she was. "What on earth would *you* know about it?" His voice dripped with contemptuous dismissal.

Kitty reeled back as if he'd physically assaulted her.

Mel stepped forward. "Mr. Thatcher, let's go somewhere private and I'll explain it all to you."

Somehow Mel managed to sweep Shelley and Jane out

of the room as well and abandon them the moment the door closed behind them. Thatcher was bellowing that he had the right to know just what the hell was going on and Mel was speaking quietly and leading him up the stairs to the privacy of Thatcher's remote bedroom.

"Can this possibly be true?" Jane said, still stunned.

Shelley headed for the kitchen. "I need coffee. Badly."

They found the largest cups in the kitchen and filled them to take outside. It was getting dark and something nearby was blooming with a beautiful fragrance. Sitting down on the slight rise where the wedding pictures had been taken a few hours earlier, Shelley finally answered. "If it's true, Kitty and Dwayne are the sleaziest people I've ever known."

"I think I find that easier to accept than you do," Jane admitted. "I haven't liked Kitty since I set eyes on her. But until now, I didn't have any reason to feel that way and felt sort of guilty about having such antipathy for someone I didn't even know."

"I guess if Jack Thatcher can turn up with a prenup contract, that will prove she's lying." Shelley blew across the top of her coffee, trying to get it cool enough to down a big, comforting slug of it.

Jane thought for a moment. "No, not necessarily. It might only prove that Dwayne was lying to Kitty about not signing it."

"Could Dwayne have really and truly had the hots for Kitty?" Shelley asked.

"Sure. Remember Joselyn Wossername? That woman who lived down the block from us years ago?"

"Only vaguely."

"She was downright unattractive," Jane reminded her.

"Thin cranky lips, practically no eyebrows, dumpy figure, awful hair. But men were gaga about her."

"But she had a good personality, as I recall. Made them all feel like King of the Mountain. Kitty didn't even have that going for her."

"Still, there's no accounting for other people's taste," Jane said. "If what she's saying is true, they were both such sleazeballs that they're way outside our range of understanding. The whole thing could have been a con job from the very beginning, just like Kitty said. They picked a sheltered, rich, mealymouthed victim who was being pressured to get married and if somebody hadn't bumped Dwayne off, it might have worked."

Shelley nodded. "You could be right."

"Remember?" Jane said. "We were wondering all along why Jack Thatcher was letting Livvy marry someone so gigolo-ish. Kitty and Dwayne knew they weren't socially acceptable to the likes of the Thatchers. They had every reason to suspect Jack would give Dwayne a bundle to get lost."

"White trash who know they're white trash and make the best use of it?"

Jane took a sip of her coffee. "Something like that. Even we know that sometimes you get what you want by being deliberately obnoxious. I've seen you do it."

Shelley grinned. "So true. But somehow I just can't accept Kitty's story. I suppose because it's so ugly and coldhearted."

"Yes, it's hard to connect with that kind of thinking, isn't it? But there is some evidence that Kitty's story is true. Just the fact that she put that wedding announcement in the paper is one thing. Nobody'd do that unless they knew for sure they were actually getting married."

"Didn't work that way in her case, though," Shelley said, flapping her hand at a moth that had taken a liking to her and kept trying to form a relationship with her hair.

"But only because they misjudged how desperate Jack Thatcher was to get some grandsons on the way. But there's more. Look at all the luggage Kitty brought along to the wedding."

"I'd forgotten that. I remember thinking she looked like she had enough stuff along to follow up the wedding with a round-the-world cruise."

"Me, too. I'd bet anything she'd burned her boats and has nearly everything she owns in the suitcases and her car. She *did* intend to marry Dwayne this weekend."

"But was it what Dwayne intended?" Shelley asked, taking another vicious swipe at the moth.

"Apparently so," Jane said, then frowned. "Or maybe not. Possibly he just let her think so. But why would he want her to believe it?"

"Was he double-crossing her?" Shelley wondered. "Maybe he was just stringing her along in case the wedding fell through and he came out of it as broke as ever. No, that won't play."

Jane shook her head. "I can't get a handle on Dwayne's role in this. Do you suppose he even *liked* either of them?"

Shelley shrugged. "I hardly spoke to him. But he could well have been one of those people who only like themselves. He certainly looked the part. Maybe he, too, had grand visions of little Dwaynes all over the place and figured Kitty looked like good breeding stock and Livvy could finance him."

"Or maybe he just got in way over his head with the whole scheme and didn't know what to do," Jane said irritably. "There was Kitty on the one hand, who appears to have absolutely worshiped him, which is pretty hard to dismiss even if you don't have an inflated ego. And Livvy on the other hand, who was reluctantly willing to provide him with cash, luxury, and social standing."

"You're saying he was spineless?"

"Probably. And maybe just too stupid to carry it off. Maybe he really did blurt out something about wanting Kitty instead, and Livvy lost her head. Imagine if you didn't really want to marry the guy to begin with, and then, while you're still in your wedding dress, he hits you with the news that he prefers a drip like Kitty. Add to that how utterly, horribly stiff-upper-lip and repressed Livvy is . . ."

"Mount St. Helen's . . ." Shelley said. "KA-BOOM!"

Chapter 22

"I can't stand this moth anymore. Let's go back inside," Shelley said.

As Jane hoisted herself wearily to her feet, she said, "Don't you wonder what she might have in all that luggage?"

"I imagine the police have already thought of that," Shelley said.

"Still, let's just have a little peek."

They refilled their coffee cups and strolled casually down the long hall to Kitty's room. Jane put her ear to the door and couldn't hear anyone inside. She tapped lightly. No response. Shelley opened the door gingerly. The room was empty.

It appeared that police had already made a cursory, and surprisingly tidy, inspection of Kitty's belongings. Two large suitcases were open on the bed. A briefcase was open on the small table under the window. Jane hadn't seen it before. A big box from Victoria's Secret was open and full to the brim with exquisite and very sexy underwear. It all looked several sizes too small for Kitty's ample figure.

"She must be pretty good at fooling herself," Shelley said, holding up a lacy size 32 B bra. "She's got to be a thirty-eight C or it's been too long since I bought underwear."

Jane was preoccupied. "There's something missing."

"What?" Shelley said, dropping the bra back into the box.

"There was another piece of luggage. A smaller case. Brown, I think. I carried it in and noticed that it was pretty light and had something in it that sort of thumped."

They looked under the bed, in the wardrobe, and in the bathroom. There was no sign of it. "Where could she have put it?" Shelley asked.

"Maybe the thumpy thing was a makeup mirror and she took it up to Mrs. Crossthwait's room, or Livvy's."

"Let's take a look," Jane said.

"What do you think is in it that makes it so important?" Shelley asked.

"I don't know. It's just the fact that it's missing that makes me wonder."

They left the room and as they went down the hall toward the main room, they passed Kitty. She tried to make a grab at Jane's sleeve, but Jane managed to dodge her grasp with a fair degree of tact. "Jane, you've got to tell them," Kitty said. "They think I killed him. I would never have done that. I'm sure it was Livvy. You have to tell them Livvy tried to get out of the marriage at the last minute."

"I have told them, Kitty. And I'll tell them again, if you want. Now, you should really go rest. It's been a horrible day for everyone."

"They're questioning Livvy now. She'll probably confess," Kitty said. "And this nightmare will be over for some people. Like you. But not for me. Never for me."

She turned and slouched toward her room, crying again. The seat of her skirt was butt-sprung, her once-crisp suit jacket was wrinkled and lumpy. The heel of one shoe looked crooked, as if it were about to come apart. She was a mess.

Shelley and Jane went to the main room where Eden and Layla had gotten another puzzle out and were silently, doggedly working on it as if solving what the picture was might resolve the whole mess. They weren't speaking. Each had a plate of leftovers and a glass of wine at the side of the table. The cat, who had befriended Jane earlier, was sitting on the third chair, with only his head showing. Any moment now, he'd be tasting one of their dinners.

"We should get some scraps while there are some left," Jane said. "But I want to look for that suitcase first."

Errol and Marguerite were now occupying the sofa Livvy had been sitting on earlier.

"Livvy's being questioned," Marguerite said. "They let her father be with her, but not me. That's wrong. Jack's such an ass. He'll huff and puff and make everything even worse. Have you two heard this absurd story that terrible Kitty person is telling?"

Jane and Shelley nodded, but said nothing.

"It's so stupid! Nobody could have believed it. Dwayne? In love with that box of rocks? Errol, you know that's not true, don't you?"

Errol shook his head. "I don't know. I've never understood Dwayne. I don't know what made him tick."

"You didn't get along with your brother?" Jane asked softly.

"It wasn't a matter of getting along so much," Errol said. "I just always felt he was thinking circles around me. He always had schemes and plans and secret stuff going on. Sometimes he'd tell me about them when we were younger and he'd be so proud of how clever he was. But I never even got what he was talking about. It was like, I dunno, circles inside circles stuff. Real complicated. Trying to second-guess everybody."

"Are you saying this bizarre story Kitty is telling is true?" Marguerite said. "And that Livvy was even remotely inclined to *kill* someone?"

Errol blushed furiously. "No, no! Not at all. I'm just saying it's possible Dwayne was plotting something weird. He usually was. That doesn't make Livvy guilty of anything. She's more like me, I think. She just wants to get along in life, do her job, be happy, and not get into fights with anyone."

"What did Livvy say about Kitty's version of what happened?"

"That Dwayne didn't even remember who Kitty was when Livvy mentioned her as a bridesmaid."

"Do you think that's true?" Shelley asked. "I mean, that Dwayne didn't remember her? Kitty told us that she'd had a date with Dwayne and introduced him to Livvy."

Errol shrugged. "I dunno. Dwayne probably had one date with dozens of women he forgot by the next day. Right now you could tell me Dwayne said he was a secret agent and I wouldn't know whether it was true or not." He turned to Marguerite. "You must think I'm an awful person, not knowing anything about my brother. You and your sister are so close."

Jane interrupted whatever answer Marguerite might have

given. "Errol, I have a sister who is just as much of a mystery to me. I've never been able to get the hang of why she does the things she does. Sometimes it's just that way. It's no reflection on you."

Jane and Shelley made their departure. "Errol, we'll be upstairs if anybody needs us. Get yourself something to eat," Jane said.

They slipped quietly into Livvy's room, searched as thoroughly as they could without messing anything up, but found nothing. Moving on to Mrs. Crossthwait's room, it was the same story. It was just as they'd left it when they'd packed up her things and loaded them into her car.

"We might as well try the attic while we're up here," Jane said.

"I'd rather eat," Shelley grumbled, but obediently followed along.

The door was still unlocked from the last time they'd been up there. It was getting dark, however, and Jane tripped over the small rug lying just inside the room. She caught herself from falling and found a kerosene lamp to light. Holding it high, they both gazed around the room, which looked much more ominous and crowded at night.

"Look! There it is!" Jane exclaimed, crawling over a box of petrified fishing reels.

She hauled out the small suitcase and set the lamp on the floor. Shelley helped clear a free space in the middle of the room and they sat down to examine the contents. There were a couple sweaters sandwiching a scrapbook.

Sloppily etched on the cover in gold ink was the name Dwayne Hessling.

Jane shivered. "I already don't like this."

"It *is* creepy," Shelley said.

They flipped the first few pages quickly, then went back and studied them more carefully. Every page featured Dwayne. Pictures cut from school yearbooks, high school newsletters. A newspaper clipping about Dwayne being part of an amateur baseball team.

Other pictures showed him walking along the street (Captioned: *Dwayne on his way to work).* Lounging on a beach someplace. Waving to someone off to his left from a boat *(A party in Evanston).* Getting into his car *(Dwayne leaving my apartment).* Shoveling snow off a driveway with a couple other young men. Opening the door of a shop.

Shelley was frowning. "These last shots are all weird somehow. What is it about them?"

"None of these pictures are posed," Jane said, staring at Shelley. "He isn't looking into the camera in any of them."

Shelley nodded solemnly. "He didn't know they were being taken."

They huddled a little closer and looked at the third to the last page. It was a photo of Dwayne and Kitty standing next to each other. But the backgrounds didn't match. It was a composite of two pictures that had been cut and carefully fitted together.

It was captioned, *Dwayne and me on our first date.*

The second to last page had a marriage license application form. Kitty's part had been filled out and signed by her. Dwayne's part was also completed, but his signature was in the same ink and handwriting as Kitty's.

And on the last page, a cigarette butt had been glued to the page. The caption read, *The cigarette Dwayne smoked after the first time we made love.*

Shelley shuddered. "That's revolting."

Jane frowned. "And it's not true."

"How on earth would you know?" Shelley asked, laughing nervously.

"Because one of the few times Livvy and I had a planning meeting, I asked her about smoking. Whether I should have ashtrays out at the lodge. She said it didn't matter, even though neither of them smoked, and went on to say that Dwayne was about the only person she'd ever known who'd never even tried smoking because he'd made some kind of deathbed promise to his grandfather."

"But Dwayne was a con man. I wouldn't believe anything he said."

"You're right about that. But Shelley, look at this book. It's sick. It's something like demented fans of famous people put together and then go shoot their idols. She followed him around, taking pictures of him when he didn't know it. All these pictures were taken where there were several or many other people around and he wouldn't notice her lurking in the area with a camera."

"She was stalking him," Shelley said. "She made up the whole fantasy and convinced herself it was true. Until she actually saw and heard him marry Livvy. The fantasy dissolved, if only for the moment it took to stab him. And . . . ! And that's why she trashed Dwayne's room. The fantasy was under severe duress. It was crumbling. It was her warning to him."

"We have to take this to Mel," Jane said.

"In a second. Jane, how could this have anything to do with Mrs. Crossthwait? Surely there aren't two people here who are as flat-out insane as Kitty. What possible reason would she have invented for killing the seamstress?"

"It wasn't invented," Kitty said from the doorway. "She knew I was pregnant."

Jane's heart leaped into her throat. She and Shelley had been sitting with their backs to the door. They both turned quickly. Now Kitty was standing on the little rag rug, holding a shotgun pointed at them.

"You couldn't be pregnant," Jane blurted out. Shelley pinched her arm. Hard.

Shelley spoke soothingly. "Where did you get that gun, Kitty?"

"Right here by the door. You were so busy saying wicked things about me that you didn't hear me come in."

"It's not loaded, you know. Hunters don't put their guns away loaded," Shelley said.

"Maybe so. Maybe not," Kitty said, smiling. "You don't know that and neither do I. But we'll soon find out. You interfering bitches! I've been listening to you and you're wrong. And you're evil."

"No, Kitty, we're not evil, and neither are you. You're just . . . confused. You need help and we want to help you," Jane said.

The door behind Kitty seemed to have a shadow that was moving.

"You don't want to help me. Nobody wants to help me. And nobody can. Dwayne's dead. Livvy killed him. And everybody's blaming me."

The shadow resolved itself into the shape of Errol Hessling. He put his finger to his lips, then made a yak-yak motion to keep her talking.

"That's just because they don't understand," Jane babbled, tearing her eyes away from Errol. "You can explain it. We'll help you. We really will. Officer VanDyne is a friend of mine. He'll listen to what I say."

Errol was crouched down, creeping up behind Kitty.

Kitty tossed her head. She didn't have the gift for doing it gracefully. "You won't help me. You're just a couple of dried-up old prunes. You don't know anything about me. Anything about Dwayne. Anything about love."

Errol was making a motion with his thumbs telling them to move apart as far as they could.

They tried to obey—oozing away from each other without appearing to move.

"But we do know, Kitty," Shelley was saying, easing away from Jane at an almost glacial pace.

"Quit looking behind me like there's somebody there," Kitty said. "I'm not stupid. I won't fall for a dumb trick like that. You bitches think you're so damned smart! Well, I'll show you who's the smart one—"

Errol nodded, then shouted, "*Move!*"

He grabbed the end of the braided throw rug and jerked it hard.

Shelley and Jane flung themselves in opposite directions and Kitty came down like a load of bricks.

The butt of the gun hit the floor, blowing a hole in the roof.

Chapter 23

"Did he pay you?" Shelley asked as Jane came into the room.

Jane tossed a check down on the bed so it showed up beautifully in the shaft of morning sunshine. "He not only paid me, he gave me an extra five hundred dollars. I think Livvy and her father had a little talk."

"Perhaps being married, widowed, and nearly arrested in the same afternoon gave the girl a bit of a spine," Shelley said. "If it didn't, nothing ever will."

There was a tap on the door. "Come in," Jane called.

Layla and Eden crowded into the tiny bedroom. "We just came to say good-bye," Layla said. "This was the most awful few days of my life, but you ladies made it bearable. And you solved the murders as well. If I ever have occasion to get married again, I'll call on you."

"Don't you dare!" Jane said, hugging Layla. "Go home to your babies."

Layla ducked out, but Eden sat down on the end of the bed. She glanced at the check, not even bothering to disguise her interest. "That's all he paid you? The old skinflint."

"It's the final payment," Jane said. "The second half."

Eden nodded. "Then it's not so bad. You earned every penny. And more. You kept poor Livvy from going to jail. Kitty actually had me convinced for a while that Livvy might be a murderer."

"We considered it, too," Jane said. "But Shelley hit the nail on the head without knowing it when she said Kitty had an amazing capacity for fooling herself. But we had no idea until we saw that scrapbook that it was a pathological ability. If you'd seen that book, it would have been obvious to you, too. And if Errol hadn't literally yanked the rug out from under Kitty, we'd have been shot."

"What was Errol doing up there?" Eden asked.

"He said he saw Kitty go upstairs and wondered why," Shelley said. "Then he started thinking about what a sneak Dwayne was, and how if Dwayne and Kitty really had been an item, she might be the same sort of person. Or worse, as it turned out. Anyway, he got worried about us and crept upstairs to see what was going on."

"Do you suppose she really was pregnant?" Jane asked. "Not by Dwayne, but by someone else."

Eden looked at her in astonishment. "And I was thinking you were such a good snoop. Didn't you think to look in her bathroom wastebasket? Lots of little wrappers that tampons come in. I assure you, she's not pregnant. But she sure is loony. I suspect she thinks she's expecting and poor old Mrs. Crossthwait yapping about how she'd gained weight made her think the old dear knew her 'secret.' "

Shelley said, "I've heard of false pregnancies. Didn't

Bloody Mary Tudor have one of those? Really believed she was pregnant and even swelled up and looked like it?"

Jane said, "Yes, I've read that, too. Kitty did look like she was about five months along, come to think of it. I bet you're right. Isn't it amazing what your mind can do to your body?"

"Has your boyfriend learned anything more?" Eden asked Jane.

"Enough to convince him that Dwayne, sleazy as he was, had nothing to do with Kitty," Jane said. "Livvy says she met him when they both were present at a minor car accident and they stood around waiting and chatting until the police could get their statements. So Kitty's story of introducing them when she was out on a date with him was a lie.

"Officer Smith called Thatcher's attorney, with Thatcher's permission, who confirmed that there *was* a prenuptial agreement signed and he had a copy. If they had divorced, Dwayne wouldn't have gotten cut off without a penny. He'd have had a modest alimony for three years. And whether they had children or not, he would not inherit her estate if she died first. It also allowed for a generous allowance for him as long as they were married."

"Tell Eden about the landlady," Shelley said.

"He also had an officer in Chicago interview Kitty's very snoopy landlady," Jane said obediently. "She says Kitty never went out at night. Never got phone calls. The police are convinced that the whole affair with Dwayne was made up."

"But *she* believed it," Shelley said. "I think she was so far around the bend that she honestly convinced herself he was in love with her. That they were having an affair and he'd dump Livvy before saying their vows."

"And when the ceremony was over, and he was officially married to Livvy, it must have been a horrible assault on her whole elaborate fantasy—which she refused to recognize as a fantasy," Jane added. "I suppose she thought if she killed him she could maintain it."

"And she nearly got away with it. Her story, as I heard it, was pretty convincing," Eden said. She stood up, gathering her purse, sunglasses, and car keys. "Well, I'm off, ladies. I'm glad I got to meet you both. You did a great job in terrible circumstances."

After hugs were exchanged and Eden departed, Jane looked around the room one more time to see if there was anything she'd forgotten to pack. If she missed it now, it was going to be gone forever. She wouldn't come back to the lodge for any amount of money. "Okay, I think I've got everything," she said. "Shelley, what's in that big paper sack?"

"Sheets," Shelley said smugly. "Linen sheets. I found a moment early this morning to chat with Jack Thatcher and learned that his father left the building and land to him, but the contents of the lodge to Uncle Joe. So I spoke to good old Uncle Joe. Money changed hands. And I now have a nice collection of antique linen sheets and pillowcases. Larkspur overheard us haggling and talked him out of a bunch of old vases he'd found somewhere. By the way, Larkspur said to tell you goodbye and he'd get back in touch when we all escaped this place."

"So you got a treasure. Larkspur got a treasure. But nobody got *The Treasure,*" Jane said, putting the check from Jack Thatcher into the zippered compartment of her purse.

She slung the purse strap over her shoulder, and took a last look in the bathroom. Their suitcases and Jane's collection of notebooks were already in the station wagon. They walked out of the room and Jane allowed herself the luxury of pulling the door closed hard enough to qualify as a good, solid slam.

The doorknob came off in her hand and fell on her foot. The door bounced back open.

Jane screeched, dropped her purse, and sat down on the floor, hugging her foot and whimpering.

"Oh, come on. Don't be such a sissy," Shelley said. "You're getting soft in your old age."

Jane drew a long breath and said, "It weighed a ton. I think I've broken a toe!"

"Jane, don't be silly. You can't break a toe with—" She'd picked up the doorknob and was hefting it in her hand. "This *is* heavy. Too heavy."

Shelley went back in the bedroom and held the doorknob in the shaft of light that had so recently illuminated Jane's check.

"Stop sniveling and come look at this," Shelley said.

Jane got up, tested her foot, and limped over.

"Look inside the back of it where the shaft went in. Get the light in there."

Jane gazed at the doorknob for a moment. "It can't be—"

"Oh, yes, it can," Shelley said. "I believe what we've got here is your average solid gold doorknob that's been painted black. Close your mouth. You look adenoidal."

"The box of doorknobs in the attic . . ." Jane muttered. "Uncle Joe kept them, so he could put them back someday and take these away with him."

* * *

Cars were being loaded up in the front drive. A uniformed officer was preparing to drive off Mrs. Crossthwait's Jeep to parts unknown. Jack Thatcher, surprisingly subdued, was loading the trunk of his car, which was blocking Jane's. "No, Daddy. That goes in the backseat," Livvy said firmly. He put the dress box in the backseat without a word. Iva and Marguerite were sitting in their vehicle, waiting while Uncle Joe unceremoniously flung their suitcases in their trunk.

"Just one thing puzzles me still," Shelley said. "The door to the attic was unlocked when we first looked in there and locked later. Who did that?"

"Uncle Joe," Jane said.

"How do you know?"

"Because I accidently told him we'd been in the attic when I mentioned that he could use the dolly in the attic to carry Mrs. Crossthwait's sewing machine up the stairs."

"Oh, of course!" Shelley said. Glancing around, she asked, "Where's Mel?"

"He left about an hour ago to have a chat with Gus Ambler on his way back home."

Jack Thatcher finally pulled away, freeing Jane's car.

"Ready to go?" Shelley asked.

"Almost," Jane said.

She got out of the station wagon and walked over to Uncle Joe, who was still abusing luggage, and tapped him on the shoulder.

"Yeah?" he said.

She reached in her purse and pulled out the doorknob.

"This fell off my bedroom door. I'm sure you don't want to lose it."

He put out his hand and a slow smile spread over his